Yielding To Unfulfilled Desires Vol 1

COREY BRYANT

Yielding To Unfulfilled Desires Vol 1

COREY BRYANT

Foreword

Introduction

Why do people choose to bite the forbidden fruit? Maybe because we're told not to. Ignoring all red flags, we bite into the fruit of our desires, which isn't bad. Unless the desires are somewhat forbidden. Like betrayal, stemming from lust, infidelity, and pure disloyalty. Sneaky things or the thrill of the challenge is very enticing! The author, in which would be me, Corey Bryant, created these stories while incarcerated in the Alabama DOC [for 27 years straight to be exact]from pure imagination and as a form of escape. As well as exercising the gift from God in which I discover in the belly of the beast.

Prologue

Book 1 "Hey Lover Hi Friend

"I can't believe you fucked her! Oh my God! You really fucked her! You slept with Tisha!" Screamed Beverly, putting emphasis on slept. "Tisha is like my fucking niece, and you had sex with her!" "Damn Beverly, I apologize, but.. Tisha is grown. And what is the problem?"I asked Beverly. She is bugging out on the fact that I had sex with Tisha, when it shouldn't even be a topic of our conversation. It ain't like Beverly and I are a couple, or even fucking.. We're just good friends. And she is acting the fuck up! "Yeah she's grown but.. But." "But what Beverly?" I asked wondering is my instincts on point, as I stand here feeling the heat coming off of Beverly. Actually feeling two kinds of heat. The kind you feel when someone like your woman is mad at you. And the other kind of heat! Sexual! Unadulturated sexual heat! Sexual energy you feel when you and an attractive person are in a room together and the both of you know that the obvious is on the other's minds, and the tension is so thick in the air, you can cut it with a knife! "What's up Beverly?" Still edging Beverly on as I step a little closer, closing in the gap causing our distance to go from casual distance to intimate distance. And the temperature in the room began to rise. "I mean.. What's wrong? Talk to me." I said in a low tone. Voice getting husky because of the sexual tension and frustration I'm feeling. "What's really going on?" By this time, me and Beverly are face to face which don't last but a couple of seconds because now we are both yielding to an unfulfilled desires, by attacking each other.

Introduction to Yielding to Unfulfilled Desires...

W hy do people choose to bite the Forbidden fruit? Maybe because we were told not to. Ignoring all red flags, we bite into the fruit of our Desires; which isn't bad, unless the desires are somewhat forbidden. Like betrayal, stemming from lust, infidelity, and pure disloyalty. Sneaky things or the thrill of the challenge is very enticing! The author, in which would be me, Corey Bryant, created these stories while incarcerated in the Alabama D.O.C (for 27 yrs straight to be exact) from pure imagination and as a form of escape. As well as exercising the Gift from God in which I discovered in the Belly of the Beast!

Book 1 "Hey Lover, Hi Friend"

Prologue

"I can't believe you fucked her!! Oh my god!! You really fucked her!! You slept with Tisha!", screamed Beverly, putting emphasis on slept. "Tisha is like my fucking niece, and you had sex with her!!" "Damn Beverly, I apologize, but...Tisha is grown..and what is the problem?"I asked Beverly. She is buggin out on the fact that I had sex with Tisha, when it shouldn't even be a topic of our conversation. It aint like Beverly and I are a couple, or even fucking...we're just good friends. And she is acting the fuck up! "Yeah she's grown but...but." "But what Beverly?" I asked wondering is my instincts on point, as I stand here feeling the heat coming off of Beverly. Actually feeling two kinds of heat: The heat you feel when someone like your woman is mad at you. And the other kind of heat! Sexual!! Unadulterated sexual heat! Sexual energy you feel when you and an attractive person are in a room together and the both of you know that the obvious is on each other's minds, and the tension is so thick in the air, you can cut it with a knife! "Whats up Beverly?", still edging Beverly on, as I step a little closer, closing in the gap, causing our distance to go from casual distance to intimate distance. And the temperature in the room began to rise. "I mean...what's wrong? Talk to me.", I said in a low tone. Voice getting husky because of the sexual tension and frustration I'm feeling. "What's really going on?" By this time, me and Beverly are face to face, which don't last but a couple of seconds because now we are both yielding to unfulfilled desires, by attacking each other.

Chapter 1 "We aint going steady"

"Heeey sweetie!", said Beverly, as I got in the car with her on our lunch break. We sat there and talked, googly eyeing each other, like a couple in love. We conversated for a while until we decided to get out of the car and walk around the parking lot, hand in hand. Then at one point, I'm hugging/holding her from the back, kissing her on her neck and ears, caressing her hips...in the parking lot! We don't care! That's what people do when they're in love! Put in on display and let the world know! She turns around and kisses me. "I love you.", said Beverly. "I love you back.", I said as I leaned in to kiss her. Then a horn blows. "Beep, Beep, Beeeep!" "Courtney!! Courtney!!" I look up and its Tisha blowing her horn at us, like shes going crazy! Blowing her horn, hollering my name, and hanging out the window with a pistol pointed at me! "Coourtneey! I know you see me! Make that your last kiss! I told you not to fuck with me!!" "Beep, Beep!" The horn, then the gun went off at the same time. "Booom!" Then I woke up! I was dreaming! Actually, I jumped up! "Courtney..Courtney! You ok?", asked Lisa, who was laying in my bed with me. "Huh? Are you straight?", asked Lisa again, as I was leaning on one elbow, looking crazy. "You must was having a nightmare?" I looked at her for a second, still kind of dazed, wondering why was I dreaming about Beverly, and was I talking in my sleep?! "Was I tripping in my sleep?...Talking and shit?" "Mmhmm.", said Lisa, as she gave me a leery look. "What I said?" "I don't know...What you're scared you said some bitch name?" Now she's tripping, because Lisa is just a jump off, and she knows this! Ever since Carolyn broke it off with me, I haven't been into the relationship thing. All I've been doing is having fun, fucking them, and leaving them! Not really leaving them, but I let it be known, off the intro, that I'm not into no serious relationship or commitment type of thing. Living the single life like Cameo! "You already know what's happening Lisa so don't go there!" "I already know what's happening? Well tell me what's happening then Courtney?" Laying back into the pillows, gathering my bearings, I answered, "We just fucking!" Lisa just sat there looking. "So if I said some bitch name, you shouldn't be mad." "Is that right?" said Lisa, leaning back as she bucked her eyes. "Yeah.", I answered. "So if I say another man's name while I'm in bed with you, you wouldn't get mad?" "Nope.", I said to Lisa, even though I'm lying. "That's bullshit, and you know it Courtney." "Cut the bullshit, what did I say?" A brief pause..."You kept saying, I love you to somebody...You didn't say no name or at least I couldn't understand you. Then, the next 30 to 45 seconds later, the alarm went off and you jumped like somebody had a gun at you!" The horn Tisha was blowing, was my alarm clock and probably the gun going off, that Tisha was pointing at me. Something external from your sleep, mixing in with your dream. "Who was at you bay?", said Lisa massaging my back, as I sat on up. Putting my boxers on, sliding my feet in my house shoes, I headed to my bathroom, to handle all hygenial duties. "Oh, so you aint gone tell me?", asked Lisa. "Nobody...I don't even remember the dream Lisa." All the time, she making me relive the dream, and try to decipher the meaning. "Yeah right.", said Lisa, "And you don't remember who you were telling that you love them?" I turned around and walked on that one. Heading through the bathroom door, and turned around and said "You.", and shut the door. I can hear her sucking her teeth through the door saying "Yeah right." Lisa and I already had an understanding about our relationship...or involvement. However you want to look at it, we're just cut friends. Friends with benefits. Just fucking! Lisa looks good; stands about 5'6", red-bone. Weighing about 165-170 Lbs, size 12. Curves in the right places, with a fat bubble butt! She had a great a career as a nurse, living good. I just didn't want to be her man! I was about to get in the shower when Lisa knocked on the door and came in butt naked, brushing past me to get in the shower. "I have to bathe before I go to work too.", said Lisa. I just looked at her as she got in my shower adjusting knobs. "This isn't hot enough. Aahh! This is just right.", said Lisa trying to look all sexy, face turned up toward the shower head, letting the water run down her face and crinkly long hair to her shoulders. Back arched, poking her ass out, as she takes the rag and squeeze soap down her neck, making it flow down her spine into the split of her butt. Now, I know what she's trying to do, that is get her some more dick before she goes to work, in hopes of pussy whipping me into not going to work, call in sick, and she do the same. Not going to happen! Well...calling in sick isn't going to happen, but give her some more dick...she got it! Standing behind her, she looking all exotic turned me on! So I did what I know best and that is to turn up! I grabbed the body wash and a bath cloth and soaped it down and started washing my tool, standing behind Lisa, watching how the soap was still running down her crack, made me go into a zone! Dick started getting hard as I was still soaping it, with my rag; I slowly started masturbating looking at Lisa! Hand raising it to its full 9 inches, Lisa looked back at the dick and then looked at me in my eyes and grabbed it. "Don't play with me!", said Lisa, obliging to her desires. I grabbed her by her cheeks and ran it deeply in her! She reached back and grabbed her cheeks and bust it open, and I grabbed her by her hair and shoulders thrusting hard! Pelvis to ass cheeks, "Sissss, that's what I'm talking about! Ooo Courtney!" Now, Lisa was a tough bitch on site, fuck game incredible! She almost dancing like the red girl from the twerk team on my dick! She already looking like her. But me, being me, that shit don't matter because I'm not falling in love with her, I'm a dawg!! Trying her best to pussy whip me, Lisa reached down and grabbed her ankles and started grinding on me, looking me in my eyes, biting her bottom lips! "Fuck me baby...ooo...dats what I'm talking about!...Fuck me harder.", said Lisa, rolling her eyes to the back of her head. Looking and sounding all sensual and sexy, made me really get in dog mode! Just when I was about to nut, I pulled my dick out and jacked and skeeted all over her butt! We in she shower, so the water is washing all of my unborn off Lisa, down the drain. Lisa being the freak that she is, plus add to the fact, that she is on a mission to lock me down, she turned around and dropped to her knees, and started giving me some head. Now really, I wasn't into it. I wanted to go ahead and shower, and get ready for work. It was already a Monday. A blue Monday! "Hold it Lisa...hold up." She didn't listen, she just kept on sucking and licking until my soldier stood all the way back in attention. "Fuck me one more time.", said Lisa wrapping her right leg around my waist. "Fuck it!" I thought to myself as I went in on Lisa. After we got through, both of us tired, we quickly showered and got dressed. "I'm tired! I don't even feel like going to work now! It's Monday too!", said Lisa, looking at me, hoping that I would say

"Fuck work, let's lay up Lisa!" Not happening. "Woman you better go on to work, cause I'm going!", I said to Lisa, putting my shirt in my pants. She didn't like that, cause she rolled her eyes at me. I see she had put her other clothes and panties in an overnight bag she had brought with her, along with her other toiletries. I had to check her awhile back for leaving her stuff at my place. Sly way leaving panties in my dirty hamper. Leave her toothbrush in my tooth brush holder. My daddy told me about all of that, a long time ago! How a woman be done sly way moved in with you, before you know it! When I did speak with her about the situation she kind of got an attitude. "What?...You have other women over here?" and I answered "Yes!" She couldn't trip, because she knew what level our relationship was on. So, when she did come over, she came prepared to take her belongings with her. Don't get me wrong, I'm not against being in a steady relationship, shacking up with a woman, marriage, or whatever. But when me and Carolyn separated, I had vowed to be a bachelor forever! Me and Carolyn, I guess you can say we hurt each other. I ain't gone lie, I took advantage of a blessing! Carolyn was a good woman. A short version (5'2") of Mary J. Blige! From her eyes, hair, lips, shape, the whole nine! But me, with an insatiable appetite, I cheated on Carolyn constantly! It wasn't the sex because she's a great lover. It was me! But I was there for her when she needed me and was there for me...for a minute. That's until the storms of life came. I had lost my job, due to some baby mama drama! I have a son, by my high school sweetheart, Tonya. My son was about 12 at the time Tonya had got in the habit of coming to my job, acting the fuck up! She was mad because the thrill was gone, but was using my son. Just like the rapper Pimp C said on "Diamonds up against that Wood". "Wicked women using children trying to live on, wanna try to hurt and hate, mad because the thrill is gone!" She would come up there acting all ghetto and shit! At the same time, I was working at Turner Broadcasting, an IT specialist. I had been warned a couple of times about Tonya coming up there like that. So I told her about it and she said she wouldn't do it anymore, she was sorry, etc. But just as soon as I back up off her, giving her space you know..stop fucking her, she goes ballistic! She might pop up on my job, stalk me, till I come to my car. She'll come in the building, find the office and go crazy! "Are you going to give me some money? Yo son need some shoes!" Before I can even answer, she'll go off. "Fuck it then nigga! You making all this money! I'll tell you something! I'll put yo ass on child support!" So Carolyn has a cousin that work there and she was telling her about the episodes. When Carolyn asked me about it, I would tell her what happened. "Let me ask you something Courtney.", said Carolyn. "Okay...what's up Carolyn?" "Are you still messing around with that woman?..Be honest." And I would look her dead in her eyes and lie. "Noo!" She would look at me, for an extra couple of seconds, and just shake her head. Women intuition was telling her otherwise. True, I was still having sex with Tonya on and off, but it was getting old quick. The last episode with Tonya was the final straw that broke the camel's back! Tonya, with her ratchet ass, came up on my job one day, clowning about another woman like me and her was a couple and I had done her wrong. One of Tonya's partners saw me at the club Twists, over in Buckhead one night, putting my game down on this chic named Alexis, and later on she saw us as at the Marriott. Little did I know, Tonya hates Alexis! In the city of Atlanta, the ratio of women is 20 to 1! Bachelor's Heaven, a player's paradise on earth! Out of all these women, it's hard to miss! But it's easy to miss your ex-girlfriends enemy, unless you already know her. To make a long story short, Tonya busted up in our office, with her hoochie momma shorts up her ass, heels on, and cut the fuck up! "How the fuck you gone mess around with Alexis?! A bitch that hates me!" said Tonya very loudly! I had to get up and escort her out of the office. People were looking from their cubicles, scared as hell. Particularly the white people. "Why doesn't he keep her on a leash?", said one of my coworkers named Cindy. "What did she say that for? What that white bitch say about me?" "She didn't say nothing, come on!", I told Tonya, grabbing her by the arm. "Nigga let me go! I heard that bitch!", said Tonya, snatching away from me. "Tonya lets go!", I said, trying to grab her arm again, and she turned around and started swinging on me. "Don't touch me!", said Tonya, and kicked her heels off and ran into Cindy, "Courtney, you fucking whitebread too?" said Tonya, as she was holding Cindy by the hair punching her. "Oh my God! Help!", screamed Cindy. I grabbed Tonya's wild ass and pulled her off Cindy, but she still had her hair. A couple of my coworkers helped me pry her hands loose. "Let me go Courtney!", screamed Tonya as I picked her up and carried her out the door. Security came in and I let them knew I had her. The halls were packed with people wanting to see what was going on. I got her to the parking lot and Carolyn's cousin was out there. "Courtney you shouldn't keep putting yourself in harms way!", said Carolyn's cousin. "Fuck you bitch! You don't know what you're talking about! Youuu are about to be in harm's way in a few fucking seconds!", said Tonya walking towards Carolyn's cousin. I grabbed her. "Won't you calm the fuck down!?", I hollered. "Why you always come to my job with the bullshit?!" "Oh so you taking up for this wench!!?", said Tonya. "I know you didn't!", said Carolyn's cousin, about to walk towards Tonya, until someone grabbed her. Now the police is pulling up and out comes Cindy and some more white people going to the police. "That's her right there!", said Cindy as she pointed at Tonya. Cindy signed a warrant on Tonya, and she went to jail. When I went back to the office, my boss man called me in his office and gave me my walking papers. Fired me! When I got home, Carolyn met me at the door, and smacked the shit out of me! I calmed her down, but to no avail, she couldn't take it no more, so she left me! The part where she hurt me at, is she wouldn't talk to me about the situation or nothing. So after a while, I said, "Fuck it! I'll just be a bachelor for life!"

***

Chapter 2 Monday Morning.

Lisa and I left my spot, heading to our cars in the parking deck. Lisa wants to walk to my car and talk and hug all on me like a couple. "What are you doing tonight?", asked Lisa. "Resting.", I said, bursting her bubble. She didn't like that, because that's when she stopped hugging on me and started halfway frowning. "Yeah right... you'll probably be at Magic City!", said Lisa. "I don't know..that bitch sho jump on Mondays!", I said, as I paused for effect before opening my car door. That's when she stepped back, putting her hands on her hips. "Courtney...I mean why do you do this?" "Do what Lisa?" "Try to treat me like I'm some kind of slut or something! I mean... if we really, really tried..and you stopped trying to handle me like I'm your hoe, we can make this work.", said Lisa, faking with the emotional quiver in her voice. It didn't move me, because I know she running game. A lot of times those tears ain't real. No, she's not crying yet, but if I sit here long enough, she'll turn up! That's why I nipped it in the bud. "It's working already Lisa." I said, as I crunk my BMW up and dropped the top and crunk my music up. Rocko's old song was on. "We just be coolin, we ain't going steady." Perfect timing, I thought to myself, as I turned the volume up, and bobbed my head with my Ray Bans on. As I was pulling off, Lisa was still looking at me as she walked to her Range Rover. I blew a kiss at her, and she gave me the middle finger. "Fuck you Courtney! Which yo sheisty ass!" I just smiled. I don't know why Lisa is acting like that. Then again, yes I do. I'm 38 years old, single, handsome, light skinned brother. 5 feet 9. Weighing about 200 Lbs. I hit the gym about 3 times a week. I'm not just ripped all the way up, but you can tell I work out. Drug free. Well, I smoke a lil weed, but that's nothing. I got a great job at At&T downtown Atlanta, Georgia, and on the side, I install electronic stuff at peoples businesses and homes. I do computer networking, fiber optics, IT work. So I make good money, and I stay sharp. I love to dress clean and then I live in a condo, at midtown. The only thing, I have 3 kids, by three different women. But they're well taken care of. Two sons and one daughter. All of them are grown, or almost grown. My daughter the youngest at 15. So of course, she would try to lock me down. To top it off, I'm slangin dick. Like I'm a youngster. Monday morning traffic, in downtown Atlanta is hectic! So while I'm sitting in traffic, I mess around with the radio and stumble up on some old school Morris Day and the time. "7-7-7-9311." I hit the volume to listen to Morris Day blow his old hit. One of my childhood favorites. Plus it puts me all the way in the mack-mode. The building I work in is full of women! All types! Black, white, Asian, Hispanic, whatever! So even though it's Monday, I always look forward to going to work. I try not to fraternize with coworkers, or have on the job. Romances, but hey...it becomes difficult. Yes it becomes very difficult when time you hit the building, some sexy ass woman (young or old), titties poking out all perky and shit, ass poking out. Looking all firm! Smelling good, lips all glossed up, hair whipped and freshly done with "Come fuck me heels on.", "Come fuck me." in their eyes!!! Shit, I got to hurry up and get to work!

Heading into my work building, I discreetly admire myself off of the glass on the building. "Damn um fly!", is what I say to myself. I got on a black Polo purple label button down, polo jeans, and some mid-cut Polo boots. Oh, and not to forget my fresh haircut! Temple blended fade with the waves, Ray Bans on. I'm fresh. "You still look the same Courtney!", said Beverly my coworker. "Oh..hey Beverly. You caught me halfway flexing, huh?" "Yeeah! You was so caught up you didn't see me coming.", laughed Beverly, as we walked in the building. "I sure didn't. But how are you feeling this morning?" "Ugh! Monday morning.", said Beverly as she rolled her eyes. "But I'm okay, I'll make it. And you? How was your weekend?" "My weekend was straight. Just need me a lil rest though." And that was the truth. After fucking Lisa last night and this morning. And clubbing Saturday. "I bet you do need some rest! What you clubbed all weekend?", asked Beverly. "A little...I went to club Twist, over in Buckhead Saturday..had a date Sunday. Well not really a date, I had company." "Uh huh.", said Beverly as she rolled her eyes, and smiling as we stepped on the elevator. "What?", I asked Beverly returning her smile. "I ain't said nothing Courtney, just laughed at you!", laughed Beverly. "Ohh okay." If I wouldn't have been thinking on terms of "my friend/coworker, Beverly." I would've sworn I caught a small glimpse or tone of jealousy radiating off of her! Naawl, Bev's my friend. She likes to meddle at me, in ways of almost flirting. But I don't take her the wrong way. She likes me, but I'm not trying to look at her in that manner. Oh, she's an eye catcher. Brown caramel skin, standing about 5'2"/5'3". About 145 in weight, medium length hair, almost to her shoulder to the middle of her neck.

Nice shape. Beverly works out about 3 or 4 times a week faithfully. Has a good job as an IT specialist also. Except she's a lead person in our office. Probably making close to 6 figures a year at the age of 43. A nice catch for a single mom. It crossed my mind several times, to get at Beverly. Just because. And to top the fact, that I'm a dawg. So I was sparing her. But I still stole me some looks at that lil plump ass she got. As I am doing now as the elevator door is closing. Just the thought of us being on this elevator alone, was getting my dick hard! She caught me...as usual. "What Courtney?", said Beverly, as I smoothly turned my head the other way. "Huh?..Oh nawl. I was looking at them shoes..them pumps!", I played it off smiling. "What kind of heels are these?" "Jimmy Choos?" "What do you know about heels?"said Beverly. "Well..not much. Not more than what somebody tells me." "Somebody?", asked Beverly. "Some woman?", she asked as she smiled at me. "Yeah, some women.", I said returning Beverly's smile. "So how was your weekend?", I asked Beverly, trying to thin some of this sexual tension which is building up between us. I feel it. "Oh..my weekend..it was okay.", solemnly said Beverly. "Why you said it like that?..Oh my bad! I hope I'm not being nosey.", I said, throwing my hands up in surrender. Beverly looked at me and smiled. "Nawl, you okay.", said Beverly. "I didn't really do nothing. My son went with his father this weekend. I went to one of my girlfriends' house for a couple of hours this weekend. We talked and had a few drinks. I went home and did some washing, and watched a movie or two, and that was it. That was Saturday. Sunday, I went to Church and had dinner with some members. Later on, I had a book club meeting. We're preparing for our "Annual All-Black Ball". "You have a book club?" "Yea.", said Beverly. We stepped off the elevator, heading to where we clock in at. "I write.", I told Beverly. And she stopped in her tracks, looking back at me, as if she didn't believe it. "You write?"

"Yea!", I laughed. "You must don't believe it?" "I mean it's possible but you've never told me that!" "What..you write books?", curiously asked Beverly. "Yea..fiction." "You haven't put one out yet?" "Nawl..I stopped about in the 5th chapter of a book and haven't started back yet, and I have another one that I've wrote about 100 pages on." "Oooh, okay. What are they about?", asked Beverly. "One of them is street fiction and the other one is an urban romance." Beverly stopped just before clocking in, and looked back at me in surprise. "What?", I asked, because now I'm looking surprised. Beverly laughed, "Romance? Umm..yeah right!" "What? You think I can't pull it off?", I said, as I was clocking in. "Umm...maybe. I didn't say you couldn't pull it off. I'm just curious about how it might turn out.", said Beverly looking back at me laughing. "I'll see you later Courtney." Now when somebody doubts me, that motivates me. I know I can pull it off! Truth is, after my break up with Carolyn, I haven't been motivated to write and finish the romance novel because she was my motivation. The book was loosely based on our relationship. But now, Beverly is my motivation to complete this book! That is, her doubt that I can't finish or write a romance, is a challenge to me. It's on!

Beverly

Write a romance book....Courtney?!...hmph!...Yeah right. I don't know if he can even be a romantic! Hmm..I don't know if he can or not...He might! He's such a player, I wouldn't bet on it! He has too many women. But that don't mean he can't be a romantic. That just mean he hoeish! Oh, what do I know? I'm being judgemental, according to the hearsay around this building, what's in the air about Courtney. "Courtney is fucking this girl with the all white Cadillac CTS- who works in finance." "Courtney is supposedly sleeping with the hot Latino chick that works on the fourth floor." "Girl you know Courtney was supposed to be in a relationship. With Valerie the second shift supervisor in accounting on the second floor." "Courtney this, Courtney that"..Been the talk for at least the last two years, out of the two years he's been here...Damn!! I don't know, maybe he is romantic enough, mixed with the imagination and drive to write a romance novel. If all this talk about him and his adventures with women are true, then he might have the experience from those relationships to write one. I wonder what he has going on, to stay in the mix with these women around here? I've never even looked at him like that, we're friends! I mean I'm not blind though! That's what all women have in common. We'll use our eyes just like men. We'll look, and even go into fantasyland. So, yes I find Courtney attractive and with a man like Courtney, us women know that we have to be cautious. But what is it that makes us (women) love and desire men with bad boy swaggers? Those who might be living on edge, so to speak? Well...I don't know, but I do know this: no woman wants a man, that nobody else wants! A woman loves a man, who loves women...and get's women! "Excuse me Beverly.", said Dorian, a worrisome, young white guy, who works close to me in my office. "Damn! Snapping me out of my thoughts. What is it Dorian?" "I'm sorry Beverly for the interruption, and I know you're just getting here. But did you get that email from Jonathan Friday evening?" "Ah, yes...did you?", I asked. "Well, sure, I just wanted to make sure the rest of the team got it." Now this was the type of stuff that made me mad and wanted to tell this lil boy something! Him coming in, starting Monday off on a stupid note, asking stupid questions. The email from Jonathan was actually an assignment for Dorian and the rest of us, which was six of us, was for support. In case he messes it up! "Dorian have you complied with the email? You got that Friday, so I know you're working on it, if you didn't finish it Friday." Standing there bewildered, Dorian answered, "Well no, not yet at least. I was going to ask you could you handle that for me."

Taking my glasses off, looking at him like he has eight heads growing up out of his shoulders. "Now you're taking this too far too early! I mean...You act like I don't have no work." "No Beverly I don't mean it like that!", said Dorian. "I have to go meet the contractor at 8:30 and.." "You are totally disregarding what I have to do! I guess since I'm such a team player, not to mention, lead person.." I stopped myself. "Dorian... go...Before you make me say something." "Come on Bev, could you..." I instantly froze him in mid sentence with my "You keep on and you're going to get your feelings hurt" look. "OK OK, Bev I'm gone!...Appreciate that." This little spoiled punk knew that I probably would go ahead and do it, because me being a lead person, I am not going to let my part of the department get behind! "I'm going to the coffee shop to get me a latte.", I said to myself as I got up from my desk and headed to the elevator. "Hey Bev!"said Dorian, calling me as he came from his desk. I immediately held up my hand as I got on the elevator. "Whew! I need a vacation!" As I enter the food court/coffee shop, I see this witch, Brenda, who works as a vendor-cashier peeping at me with a scowl on her face. I try to ignore her, because today is the right day for her to get cussed out! I don't know what's wrong with Brenda. For some reason she doesn't like me, she won't speak to me if and when I come in here by myself. But if someone else is around she'll put up a front and speak with a fake smile. Like now, because Lacresha from finance is here. "Hey Lacresha, hi Brenda. How are y'all doing this morning?" "Hey Beverly!", said Lacresha. "Oh..hey Bev erly.", said Brenda like an afterthought, with a fake smile, rolling her eyes, "Whaaat?", I said with a bewildered look on my face, as I watched Brenda as she rings up a customer's order. Sensing the childish tension, Lacresha attempts to cool the situation. "Hey Hon, how have you been lately?", asks Lacresha motioning with her eyes towards Brenda as if asking me, "What's up with her?" "Guurl, I've been doing okay!",

I said shrugging my shoulders, responding to her clandestine question like "I don't know what's wrong with Brenda." "Monday morning!", I laughed. "Guurl, you know it!", said Lacresha. We stood there and chitchat for a minute before we ordered. Just before we did, Courtney swaggers in, behind the Eva Mendez look alike from the 4th floor. Who he's rumored to be fucking. For some reason the air changed. Courtney came in and shook the whole atmosphere up. "Yeah right you'll just tell me anything.", said Larissa, aware of how quiet it got when her and Courtney walked in. Obviously stunting on all of us black women, because of Courtney, "Morning" all of us dry spoke in unison. "Heeey Courtney", said Lacresha, adding irons on the fire. All I could do was roll my eyes and smile. But not without Courtney noticing! He frowned, "What's that all about Bev?" frown with a smile, though right before speaking to Lacresha. "Lacresha..How you doing?" "Just fine!", said Lacresha, grinning, being messy. Brenda, forgetting all about me and Lacresha, slithered down the counter to take Courtney's order. "Hey Courtney, what will you be having this morning?" "My bad.", said Courtney. "They was in front of us. Bev, y'all about to order?" "No, they was just chit chatting.", interrupted Brenda. Clearing my throat, "Uuh...we're through, and we would like to order now.", I said in a sarcastic matter of fact kind of way. Brenda didn't like this one bit, because that smile she was giving Courtney, quickly melted away, as she looked at me like "I know you didn't." "So... what would you be having Beverly?" "Give me a small latte..and that'll be all." Going into my sarcastic, black woman mode! Lowering my eyes, twisting my lips up, and almost rolling my neck. As Brenda walks off to fix my latte she rolls her eyes at me. If she couldn't be seen, she would spit in my latte. Courtney notices the exchange and smiles at me, but continues to whisper sweet nothings in Larissa's ear, and she's purring and giggling so we can hear it. "Beverly...what's wrong with your coworker?", asked Lacresha, referring to Courtney. "I don't know... what you mean?" "How he's just..I guess you could say doggish.", said Lacresha. "Guurl,l I guess he's just being a man." It was clear that Lacresha was jealous, but no lie, even though me and Courtney was coworkers and good friends, I was a little jealous.

Chapter 3 Mask on

As I returned back to the office, with coffee in hand, I did my daily ritual of stopping by Beverly's office to holla at her, we cool. "Knock knock!", I said, as I stuck my head into Beverly's office. She looked up at me all straight face and stuff. Making my smile go away. "What's wrong? You okay?", I said, trying to hide my disappointment of not being received by Beverly in her usual warm, welcoming smiling way. At least not off the top! "Oh I'm good!", said Beverly, all of a sudden in a cheery, almost nonchalant, yet good mood. Mask on Beverly and I, not only been coworkers for 2 years, but very cool with each other coworkers for 2 years. Friends! So I kind of know when something might be wrong, but not yet totally hip to when she places her mask on. Mirroring Beverly, by placing my mask on, smiling and said, "You could've fooled me for a minute. If I didn't know you, I would've thought something was bothering you just then. Are you sure you good?" Taking her glasses off laughing, "Oh...and you know me?", asked Beverly. "Well...I'm going to put it this way...I think I know you well enough to know when something is up." A brief pause before Beverly started laughing. "Nooo..I'm just kind of sleepy. This lil fool Dorian, is up to his B.S. early Monday morning.", said Beverly as she gave me the rundown on what was going on. "Then I left, before I cussed him out, to get me a latte and get down there, to be sassed by Brenda! Not really sassed....but I don't know. She don't like me! She's just a...she's a trip!" Now me having been around Beverly communicating and observing, those incidents are normal. Yeah...they'll get to her, if she allow it, but recoverable. But now my instincts is telling me something else is up. Oh well, not reading too much into it, I changed the subject in a subtle way. "Not changing the subject but Bev, you done motivated me!" "I done motivated you?", asked Beverly looking curious and smiling very hard. "Are you okay?" "Yeah, I'm straight!", I said laughing at Beverly. "So how did I motivate you?"said Beverly, rising from her desk, hand on her hips. At this moment, my friend Beverly is looking good, making me want to taste her. Motivating me now, but in a different context. Wiping it out of my mind, for now, I stopped playing with her. "You know I'm talking about my book. Finishing my book!" Shifting her pose, letting out a laugh, glad that I wasn't talking about something else. Beverly was interested. "Oh really? So when are you going to finish it? I want to read it." "I don't know, you might have to give me a minute. Give me a month or two." "A month or two?!", said Beverly. "Now you said you had five chapters already. Right?" "Right?", I answered. "I tell you what. It's the middle of March right now, and I have my annual book club ball in July. Have it ready in June. me and my book club will read it and present and sponsor it, so to speak, at my ball." With my hand on my chin looking up in the air, as if I'm thinking hard. "Hmmm, that's a bet!" Beverly and I shook hands on that. "Bet!", said Beverly. We stood there and chit chatted for about two more minutes and I left, heading back to my cubicle. I had to catch up on some work. I'm the type of person, that will do instant replays in my mind, and observe anything that's giving me a hunch about something and right now, it's Beverly. The way she looked at me, when I first went to her office, after leaving the food court-coffee shop, and then at the coffee shop even though I was all into Larissa, I felt the vibes in there. Beverly knows how I am, but I was seeing something in her eyes...like a hint of jealousy. I could be wrong, or, I could be wanting her to be jealous. Nah! But, we could be in sync with each other, because I get a little jealous when I see a man talking to her..sometimes..especially the hugs. I didn't used to be like that. Do I want Beverly for myself? Do I want to just fuck her? Or is it just curiosity of an unfulfilled desire? Damn! I got to snap out of it! Got to get back to work, but before I do, one more mental self inventory. Has Beverly motivated me to finish my book just to show her I could do it and flex my skills? "Yep." Also deep down inside, do I want to finish this book, to see can I captivate her with it? "Hah Hah...yep. Stop it Courtney! Beverly is your friend.", I tell myself as I get back to work and think about what I'm doing tonight.

Beverly

"Damn!" Courtney thinks that he knows me. He can tell that something is on my mind. I wonder if he know that it's him? He can't possibly know. But he seen through my mask. Nonsense. He ain't no mind reader. It's been bothering me all morning, that this thing is bothering me!! That is to see how Courtney and Larissa (the hot Latina) vibing like that. I mean, Courtney and I have always been friends. And after a while, we confided in each other on life issues, family, how we view things, and even relationships. But I have never let him in toonclose. But besides all of that, I shouldn't have a reason to be jealous. He has talked to me about past relationships with women outside of our workplace and current relationships. Hell..I have even given him advice on dealing with women. Answered questions and he listens to me, and my issues without passing judgement, which is a plus. "Heey Bev, what's up?" Speaking things into existence. Damn! It's Courtney. Mask on. "Heey.", I said, smiling in my normal way. "Oh okay, you done cheered up?", asked Courtney, smiling. Looking all fine and...come back girl! Snap out of it. "Yeah...I'm good. Trying to finish up Dorian's mess and catch up on mine as well. What's going on wit ya?" Uh oh! He must've caught something in me! Because he got this smoky look in his eyes all of a sudden and biting his bottom lip. "Courtney!", I said snapping him out of his lust filled daze. "Oh my bad..yeah um..had a question about this..um..troubleshooting. Troubleshooting on this assignment I got early this morning." Now, if Courtney only knew the trouble shooting I need. Oh my! My mind is everywhere and why is he looking at me like that? "Um..Beverly..you heard me?", smiled Courtney. "Oh my bad! I was trying to...see (that button down Polo fall off your shoulders and to see what you're working with under them Polo jeans, is what I'm trying to see) what assignment is this?",I asked, trying to fix my mask. You know, shift the mood. "Hold it..now Courtney...You better be glad you and I are cool, for me to stop doing what I'm doing and look into this for you.", I said smiling and rolling my eyes at Courtney. And for effect, I poked my 3600 titties out, arching my back a little more than needed, because I knew he was watching as I swiveled my chair towards the computer screen. I had on my grey skirt suit, which was kind of short. Thighs showing extra since I'm sitting down and I have a tank top on under my jacket. Let me stop. Courtney's my friend. Talking about deprived. Ever since I divorced Johnny a year ago, I haven't really been getting me none. Here and there and on occasions, but I'm not the promiscuous type. It's been 4 months since I had sex and it was with an old flame from college who I seen at homecoming. I seen him at an old school themed party and that was something. I guess you can say...it just happened. Me and Courtney are so tight that I told him about it. His response kind of throwed me, because he seemed a little jealous. Because he was like "Straight up?!" In a surprising manner and the way he got quiet and the way he was looking at me. "What?", I asked him. He was smiling, but his eyes wasn't, then he answered, "Things, don't just happen." Then I was like, "What?", and he said he was just playing, but I wasn't going to let that go, I made him explain what he meant. Then he made me explain what I meant! So, we went on and on like he was my man and I was his girl. We do that at times, but he just cares about me..I think that's what it is. All of this on my mind as I pull this stuff up on the computer screen for Courtney, and try and help him troubleshoot. "Okay Courtney. I see where the problem is." I think it's dealing with the modem on this end or their end. "And um..", I said, pausing or should I say stop because Courtney is almost leaning over my shoulder at the computer and his scent to go along with the light smell of some good cologne is intoxicating me. Or is it just the fact that he's so close to me? I'm definitely tripping! Because he has been this close to me before. "And um what Bev?", asked Courtney. "Oh,", I said and started to explain to him what I had found. "Okay Bev! Good looking out. I'm going to go ahead and handle that.", said Courtney walking off. "I'll get with you later." "Anytime Courtney." "Whew! I'm glad he's gone! I got to get it together.", I said to myself and went back to work.

Courtney

"Shit!" Beverly giving off some strong ass vibes, or am I just tripping? I got to hurry up and get back to work. Sitting down at my computer, glad nobody didn't recognize how hard my dick was. I went to work...with Beverly on my mind. She's my friend, good friend, but I'll add her to the stable. By the time I went to dwelling on that thought, my cell phone vibrated. Looking at the caller I.D. it was my cousin Trez calling. "What up bwoy?", I said, answering the call. "What up cuzzo?", said Trez. "Shit...at work trying to get this stuff done so I can get off on time. What's up wit you?" "Man, just cooling..but aye, check this out!", Trez said excitedly. "You remember them broads I was fucking with on facebook?" "Which ones?", I laughed. "The hoes out of South Carolina. I was showing them to you. Wanda is the super fine red bone who be posing for different independent magazines or some shit. You remember she was posing naked, like on a stamp, and the stamp was in a champagne glass?" "Oh.. yeah!", I said remembering the picture. "Okay...so what about them?" "What about them?! Man they'll be down here tonight!", said Trez. "Wanda was asking about you. Remember when you sent her the friend request after seeing her, and she accepted?" "Yeah, yeah, that's right!", I said. "I know..she told me y'all been chopping it up on facebook a lil bit." "Yeah! We did..but I didn't really pursue her hard for real." "Well, she pursuing you now! What's up? I just got off the phone with them." Me and Trez were always on the hunt for some women. "You already know I'm wit it cuz! I get off at five o'clock, I'll hit you then.", I said, hitting the end button on my phone and lo and behold, there's a message from Wanda through the messenger app through facebook. I already had enough live action on my phone. The message read, "Hey Courtney, haven't heard from you in a while. Well, I told Trez that me and Keosha would be in Atlanta tonight. I hope we can hook up." I immediately responded to her message letting her know Trez told me and gave her my number. After I did that, I went to her photos to amp myself up. "Damn!", I said, kind of loud, noticing Beverly was passing by my cubicle. Wanda was posing with a white, tight ass short body dress on with holes up the side. Then she had some heels on. "Girl I'm gone beat that pussy up!", I said as I strolled through her pics humming Jeezy's old song "Beat that pussy up". "Um-ugh.", clearing her throat, Beverly was looking over my shoulder! I had the phone right in front of the keyboard of my computer, with the pics on full view! "Boy, I thought you had done messed up or ran into some trouble on your computer, and here you are looking at some....some photos!", said Beverly. "Okay Beverly...my bad.", I said smiling and taking the phone off facebook. Beverly saw the pics though. Looking back at Beverly, with her nose turned up, with a smirk on her face. "I'm about to handle it Beverly." "What?", I asked Beverly, cause she still was standing there. "That's all you think about," said Beverly, walking off, referring to them pics. "Yeah, and money.", I said. I went on and got to my task at hand. "Damn, what's bugging her."

Chapter 4 Monday Night

Trying like hell to get out of this downtown traffic, slightly irritated, I did something that I had slowed down doing...I lit a cigarette. I keep them on deck for this type of stress. Anyway, for a Monday, my day was cool. Nobody didn't bother me, making me pissed off. I caught up and stayed on point with my work. I flirted good with the women. Got me a phone number from this new young chick, who works on the sixth floor. Her name is Sade. around 24-25 years old. About 5'5", brown skinned, looking like a young Natalie Cole. Hazel green eyes, gap in teeth, with a kind of short hairdo, fine body. Look like she walked right out of my dreams! I'll call her in a couple of days. Larissa, my Latina broad is ready to be smashed tonight, but I had to put her off for this new pussy, Wanda, from South Carolina. Speaking of Wanda, I need to call Trez. Now, that thought had me going through a total recall. I'm already, a thinking man, and I'll go through a review of my day, events and the feelings I had when I experienced whatever it was. Beverly! Not wanting to admit it to myself, because me and Beverly are friends. Close to the point, we call each other here and there. Not taking her the wrong way because she gives off an aura like she's with it, and a lot of guys will take her the wrong way, but today, she gave off some vibes like she's into me another way! Especially when I was catching little hints of jealousy. I don't know, but for now on, I'm going to keep my eyes open. You know, turn up my come and get me rader. As I move through traffic, dwelling on the situation about Beverly, my phone goes off. It's Trez. "What up cuz?" "What up Courtney?" "Just getting off work, navigating through this traffic, what it do?" "Nigga you already know what it do. These hoes is here!", said Trez. "Where y'all at?", I asked. "We over here chilling at Club Onyx, waiting on you." "I'm almost at the crib. Give me about 35-40 minutes. Give me an hour and I'll be there.", I said, as I moved this BMW through traffic. "That's him?", I heard a female voice in the background ask. "Yeah!..Aye cuz here she go.", said Trez, handing Wanda the phone. "Heey Courtney!", said Wanda. "Heey how you doing Wanda?", I said. "Chilling..waiting on you." "Oh yeah?", I asked. "Yeah!", said Wanda, and we talked shit for a minute, till I pulled up to the condo, it's time for me to get right.

Beverly

Entering my house, my dogs Puff and Goldie meet me at the door. I hear them barking before I put the keys in the door. "Move, before I step on y'all.", I tell the dogs. They're small ankle biters, Yorkies. "Y'all happy to see me?", I said reaching down and giving them both a rub on the head. "Hey ma..what's up?", said my son, Anthony, as I walked past the den. He was laid back on the love seat, talking on the cell phone. "What's up?", I asked. Then I backed up to give him that accusatory motherly look. He wasn't even paying attention as he spit his lil adolescent game at one of his girlfriends. "Yea boo, I was thinking about you all day. In fact, in 3rd period. So much my dick.." "Anthony!", I screamed at him, stopping him before his dirty mouth gets him grounded. "Oops! Hold on!", said Anthony cuffing his phone. "Uh..hey ma!" "Don't hey ma me Mr. What I told you about yo dirty mouth?" "I'm sorry ma. I didn't see you! I was.." "I know you didn't see me!", I said cutting my manish son off. "And have you done your homework, while you kicked all back, talking nasty on the phone?" "Ma I was just about to get started on it and my phone rung." "Okay then..so where is it?", I asked, cause I didn't see anything remotely looking like school work. "Um uum.", stuttered Anthony. "Yea I know!..um um! You need to get about your bizness first, then get on the phone. Talk all you want." "But ma.." "But ma nothing!", I said as I mean mugged him. "I'll call you back.", said Anthony. I walked on to my room, sitting my purse down. My son Anthony is a good kid, I just have to stay on him, trying to keep him from getting sidetracked. And I know that's easy for a 15 year old to get sidetracked. Kicking off my heels, and suit jacket, I sat back on my bed. "Whew! I'm kind of tired." Closing my eyes and rolling my neck around, trying to ease the tension in my neck. Picturing me getting a massage. Visualizing calm pictures, sounds and feelings help. Picturing the stress of the day and discomfort, slowly ebb away. "You feeling okay?", asked Courtney, in a low, deep sensual voice. My eyes pop open. In surprise of me fantasizing about Courtney. "Damn! My imagination is running wild! Fuck it! Not adhering to my more rationalizing part of me, I close my eyes and go back into my fantasy. His hands move down to my shoulders. Squeezing, massaging and caressing with his thumbs and fingers. Applying pressure here and there. Moving back up towards my neck. Stopping in the space there between my neck and shoulders. Easing his hands, massaging my back, breathing in my ears, whispering something. And then..my phone rings! "Damn!" Looking at the phone, it's my God niece Tisha. How ironic, she would call, and she has a thing for Courtney. How she met Courtney was through me. She seen him a couple of times while she was with me. This particular time, the time she nearly lost it, was one day I called him, putting him on a hustle. My uncle needed someone to come through and install some electronic stuff in his home. When I asked Courtney where he was located, he said he was at his mother's house, over in Adamsville, planting some flowers for her. "Planting flowers?!', I laughed. So that probably was a sight to see, because he was usually so clean and fly and he said his mother was drinking strawberry daiquiris as he was planting. "Want some?", he asked. "We're on our way.", I said. We wasn't too far from there anyway, coming from college park. I already knew where she stayed, because I took him there to get his car one day from work. Me and my god niece pulled up in her white Mercedes, he was standing there, with two flower pots in hand, with one of those tight short sleeved under armour t shirts on, some blue jeans and some knee pads on. He was sweating and slightly dirty. But he was looking very, very, delicious and cool. He always got to be cool. He had on some Dolce and Gabbana shades, and a black Atlanta Falcons fitted hat turned backwards. "Oh my god! Girl, this negro..is..ooo! He is fine! Beverly you got to hook me up!", said Tisha. "What?! I don't run no dating service. Hook yo self up." We got out the car and went and talked to Courtney. Since that day, she's been hell bent on getting with him. Now here she is on the phone just as I was thinking, umm..okay...as I was fantasizing about him. My friend. I need to get distracted from that thought. "Heey girl!", I said as I answered Tisha's call. "What's up?", said Tisha. "Just getting off of work, sitting here trying to figure out what I need to be doing. What's up?" 'Nothing. Just got off of work myself, calling to see if you wanted to go somewhere and have a few drinks or something." "I don't know girl..I need to see if Anthony had anything to eat first. I might have to cook him something.", I said, as I got up and walked back downstairs to check on Anthony. "Girl, he can cook can't he?", said Tisha. "Humph..he can do a lil something, but I don't want him messing something up. I don't want him burning my house down.", I laughed, entering the den. I noticed Anthony was doing his homework. Good! "Anthony, have you eaten anything?" "Yeah. I ate the leftovers from our Sunday dinner." "Okay.", I said as I walked off. "Got that established..He's ate. So what do you have in mind? Where you plan on going?" "I don't know...let's hit a club!", said Tisha. "Girl you know I don't do clubs! Maybe a jazz club. Tisha, you know I got to go to work in the morning!", I said. "Okay, okay Beverly. I just haven't seen you in a while and I thought maybe we can hang out a lil bit. That's all. I won't keep you out too late. Cool?" I paused for effect. "Umm..okay." "Good! Got to get you out of the house! Don't want you to turn into an old maid on me!" "Girl please! Never dat!", I said. "Will an hour be good enough for you to get yourself together?", said Tisha. "Yes, that'll be fine.", I said as I was taking off my skirt. "Okay Bev. I'll be there to pick you up." "Okay. Bye." "Bye." Placing my phone on the nightstand, after hanging up, I sat there thinking about Tisha. She's good people, but at times she can get on a person's nerves. Not to mention, she's kind of loose. So,that's why the hesitation would come into play when it comes to going out with Tisha. That's part of the reason we haven't seen each other lately. I kind of fell back. Tisha is 22 years old. Kind of young for me to be hanging out with, when I'm 40. She's cool, but she got a little more growing up to do. I've been knowing her since she was a little girl. Her aunt Janice and I been friends since we was in high school and she used to always be around when I came over or she'll be with Janice sometimes when she would come over to my house. So, I kind of adopted her as my god niece. Oh well, I guess it's okay if I step out with

Tisha...for a minute. Going to my closet to find something to wear, my phone rang. "I wonder who this is.", I said. Looking at my caller i.d., it was my ex husband Johnny. Now, I wonder what he wants? I started not to answer it, but then too, it could be something about our child. "Hello?" "Hey Beverly. How are you doing?", said my ex husband Johnny. "I'm doing okay..and you?" "Oh...I guess I'm kind of lonely." "Umm...that sounds like a personal problem Johnny." "I know..so what are you up to?" "Huh?..Well I'm about to take me a shower." "A shower?!...I wish I could come over and shower with you." "Wrong answer Johnny! Look I'm running late, so it was nice talking to you..bye.", I said and hit the end button. Not trying to be mean to him, but it's over between me and him. I laid my clothes out and went to the shower. Got to get ready for Tisha.

Courtney

After getting out of the shower, getting myself together, I checked the time to see how long it took me, or should I say how long it is taking me to get there. I kind of take pride in being prompt. "15 minutes to get to Onyx, I'm doin good.", I said to myself as I hit the door. I almost was side tracked by this white girl named Natalie, who stays in the same building. "Hey Courtney!", said Natalie. "Hey Natalie...how damn!" I had to do a double take because Natalie had on some boy shorts up her ass! And she's already one of them new phenomenon white women. A white woman who is made up like a black woman. "Whaaat?", laughed Natalie, acting like she don't know what has me staring and stammering. "You know what!", I said and turned to walk on the elevator, pressing the button. "No I don't. Tell me.", said Natalie, smiling like a chess cat, in a seductive way though. Backing up into the elevator, as the door opened, grabbing my dick and looking down at her short, shorts and said, "One day...one day soon!" She smiled, nodding her head, and walked off. "Whew!" I'm glad that she kept going and the door closed, because she can get aggressive like the white woman on Beyonce and Idris Elba's movie "Obsessed". Got to the parking deck, hopped in my car, and mashed out. Once I got to club Onyx, I was calling my cousin Trez, trying to locate them. "Aye cuzzo..where y'all at?" "Shit, where you at?", asked Trez. "In the parking lot." "Stay right there, we're coming to you." said Trez. A moment later, Trez came out the door, leading two fine ass females to the parking lot. "Damn, they ain't bullshittin neither!", I said speaking on Wanda and her friend. Trez spotted me instantly laying against my car. "What up cuz?! Here they go!", said Trez as we bumped fist and I hugged Wanda and her friend. "Heey! How y'all doing? Damn! Y'all are absolutely...stunning!", I said, as I stepped back, still holding Wanda's hand, as I admired her outfit. Body dress with colors in it like a disco ball. Red, purple, silver, shiny. And fitting in all the right places. Breaking the ice because it's already kind of awkward, being that we met through the internet. Both parties have to be careful. "Heey Courtney! How are you?", said Wanda, stressing the "You!" Letting it be known that she's not one bit bashful. "I'm cooling! Glad to be in your presence! Check this out. I know y'all don't want to stay here at the strip club. I know this nice lil jazz club, we can go to called 281 over on Peachtree. It's a cool spot." "Yea! I know where that is!", said Trez. "Is that okay with y'all?", I asked Wanda and her friend. They looked at each other, as if one was waiting on the other to decide. Wanda took the lead, "Yeah, that's cool!", said Wanda. "That's what's up!", I said as I got in the car. "Y'all just follow me!" Not even offering Wanda to ride me and her friend to ride with Trez. That might spook them. Got to keep them comfortable. They headed to their car. They was driving a silver Lexus. Looking like ES 350. And Trez headed to his Yukon and we all pulled off.

Beverly

Tisha must have a time clock or something, because she showed up at my house in exactly an hour just like she said. "Ding dong, ding dong. Ding, dong!!" She was ringing my doorbell like she was going crazy or somebody was at her. "Anthony! Anthony!!", I was hollering for my son to answer the door. "Huh?!", said Anthony. "I know you hear the doorbell!", I said. "I'm going, I'm going!..damn", Anthony cursed under his breath thinking I didn't hear him. "I heard you! What I told you about that mouth?" Walking from the top of the stairs, back to my bedroom to continue getting dressed, I heard Tisha talking to my son. "Heey Anthony!" "Hey Tisha.", said Anthony. "Where yo momma?" "She upstairs." "Beverly!", screamed Tisha. "Girl I know you ought to be ready by now!" "Coming!", I hollered back as I was coming out of my room, turning my light off. "Ooo, look at you! You trying to get picked up or something?", said Tisha teasing me about my outfit, which was kind of simple. I had on a white, short sleeve button down shirt, with a lime green skirt and some six inch heels. "No Tisha. I'm not trying to get picked up, but it looks like you are though." Tisha had on a tight black leather body dress, with holes up the side, leaving little to the imagination. To top it off, with some six inch heels on with straps running up her calf. "Well...maybe.", laughed Tiha. I went in the den to check on Anthony before we left to make sure he was doing his homework. "What's up ma? You gone?", asked Anthony, as I peeped in on him. "Yeah..you can't wait till I leave huh? Well don't let me come home and find out you haven't finished your homework!", I said. "I will ma." "And make sure you don't leave all these lights on, and set the alarm." "Okay ma." "Let's go Tisha. "Bye Anthony.", said Tisha. "Bye." Me and Tisha left and was headed out.

Courtney

The spot was kind of packed for a Monday night. I guess everybody was unwinding after work. Happy hour, or just plain bored. Then too, folks like to party in Atlanta, so it isn't strange to see people out. We found us a section in a dimly lit corner, sat down and prepared to order some drinks. "What y'all drinking?", I asked. "Um, I'll have a Remy Red.", said Wanda. "I'll have the same.", said Wanda's friend. "What about you Trez?" "Double shot Ciroc.", said Trez. "Okay..give me two double shots Ciroc, and two Remy Reds on the rocks.", I told the waitress. We talked and laughed, as we waited on our drinks, unwinding and getting better acquainted. "Excuse me for a minute.", I said, as I got up and went to the restroom. Upon leaving the restroom, I spotted my coworker Beverly and her god niece Tisha. "Damn!" Both of them was looking good, but Tisha was repping hard with that leather on! Within seconds they looked around and spotted me. "Heey Courtney!", said Beverly, as she walked up and hugged me. "What's up Bev?..Hey ah..Tisha? That's yo name right?", I said as I shook her hand. "Yeah, that's my name!", said Tisha looking me up and down. So I returned her an up and down look. "I thought you was going to get you some rest Courtney? That's what you said at work today.", said Beverly. "Yeah..I did say that.", I laughed. "But hey..what can I say? Can I buy y'all ladies a drink?" Beverly looked at Tisha and back to me. "Why sure!", said Beverly. We stepped to the bar. "What y'all drinking?" "I'll have a double shot apple martini.", said Tisha. "And I'll have a pineapple daiquiri.", said Beverly. "Coming right up.", said the bartender, who did a double take. "Courtney?! What have you been up to? I haven't seen you in a while.", said the bartender. Her name was Shan. Shan was a redbone with a mermaid shape, but with a fatter ass. I had met her at Clark University. She was in the school of nursing over there. "I just been cooling Shan. I almost forgot you worked here. I haven't been over here in awhile." "I know...let me go ahead and fix these drinks, I'll see you around.", said Shan. "Okay Shan." I made a mental note, to get back through here to get at Shan. Actually, I had got at her awhile back, but she was procrastinating, so I moved on. Becoming aware of my existing date, I kind of dismissed myself from Beverly and Tisha. "Okay Beverly, Tisha..I got to get back to my friends over here. So, I'll catch y'all later." "Okay Courtney! See you at work tomorrow...if you make it.", laughed Beverly. "Yeah...will see you later.", said Tisha, stressing "will see", and looking all suggestive. Looking back, to let her know, that I caught her subliminal message! "Okay Beverly, okay Tisha." Making my way back to the table, I hollered at dude I knew, using him as a decoy to look back at the bar, I spotted Tisha eyeing me down. Beverly wasn't looking, that's when I held up one finger, to let her know "give me a minute and I'm coming back through." She gave me a sneaky nod and smile, letting me know she acknowledged me. I sat back down with Wanda and crew. We talked and got tipsy, trying to see what the night was going to bring. "So....where shall we go from here?", I said in Wanda's ear. "Umm..I don't know. You tell me!", said Wanda grinning like Chester the cheetah. "That's easy for me.", I said in Wanda's ear. "Oh yeah?...Well I'm following your lead.", said Wanda, rising from her chair, letting me know she's ready and with whatever. "But first, let us go to the ladies room." "Cool.", I said rising from my chair. "I'm going to the men's room." As the ladies made their way to the ladies room, Tisha was coming out, and walking right up to me, sliding me a piece of paper in my hand discreetly, which I'm pretty sure was her phone number. She broke her stride for a moment and said, "What's your number?" I quickly gave her mine and she brushed up against me, and kept going, just as I did the same. I didn't see Beverly, but she was on my mind. "Damn man! Girls, girls, girls."

Chapter 5 A month later

That night after the jazz club, me and Trez took Wanda and her friend to the DoubleTree, and fucked them like some gigolos! Meaning, we were bout our business! Fucking them like we were getting paid for it. We found out Wanda, and her friend was some freaks/lovers! They wanted to get fucked in the same room and same bed! Yeah! It kind of was no surprise to me because I was reading their body language, and the way they looked at each other. They had this weird agreement that they were going to be a couple. But have an open relationship with men. But only on the basis of them sharing the dude, or they get laid together by two men. Through the whole ordeal, physical contact was to be made between the two. Whether it be holding hands, lying side by side, or kissing each other, while be fucked from the back at the same time. Or one eats the other one's coochie while they getting it in. Get totally freaked like they're on a porno flic. Which is exactly what we did to them. The next morning, we sent them on their way and I went to my crib, and Trez went to his. Beverly was right...I didn't go to work. I went home and showered and jumped right in the bed. But first, not without checking my phone, a ritual. "Damn!", I said, tripping because someone had hit me from the same number about three times back to back, and a text behind that. "I wonder who number is that?", I said to myself. Then it hit me. "Tisha's number!" To be sure, I reached in my nightstand, grabbed the piece of paper I had in my pocket and it was Tisha's number. "Damn, she hitting me up already?!" I opened the text and read it. "Waz jus callin 2 c wut u waz up 2...diggin u! :)" "Ookay!", I said to myself. Should I text her back or wait? Well, by me not really just trying to make nothing out of this, like a relationship. Nothing but a fuck, I guess I will hit her back. She wants me to move fast, so that's what I'll do, turn up with her! "Just seeing your text. In bed now tho. I will hit u later on...oh diggin u 2!! :)" I sent that text off, called in sick, turned the phone off, put it on the charger and went to sleep. When I woke up later that day, I checked my phone, and Tisha had done text me twice, after she answered my text which was a smiley face with Lol. I decided to go ahead and call her and see where her head was at. She turned out to be cool for a younger woman (22). We talked for a long time, getting to know each other, how Beverly became her god aunt and how she been told Beverly to hook her up with me. I told her Beverly never said anything to me about it. Maybe it slipped her mind, by her being so busy. Oh well, we still made it happen, because in a week's time, me and Tisha was in a room at the 4 seasons, sweating up the sheets! I knew it wouldn't take long to get the pussy, because of the way she was all on me. Now that a month had passed, I still fuck Tisha lil young pussy here and there, but I'm kind of getting tired of her. Even after getting some understanding with Tisha that we're just friends, she still be on some other shit, like I'm her man. We're not necessarily lovers. Because there is no feelings attached, not with me anyway. I almost wanted to talk to Beverly about it, but lately she's been acting kind of salty and distant. I don't know if she's like that right now with everybody, but with me she is. In fact, when she found out me and Tisha exchanged numbers that night at the jazz club, she was acting funny. When I missed that Tuesday of coming to work, that Wednesday she said something to me about it after joking with me. "Courtney what I tell you Monday night? That you were not coming to work the following day." "Yeah you was right," I answered. "Uh huh.", laughed Beverly. "And oh yeah...have Tisha been bothering you already?", said Beverly, as she turned and walked off. "What?! come here Beverly.", I got up from my desk and followed her into her office. She looked back smiling, but I noticed the usual smile that occupied her eyes was missing. "What?", said Beverly. Then I asked her what she meant by what she said. "Tisha told me she gave you her number, and you gave her yours.", said Beverly, shrugging her shoulders like "So!" and turned and faced her computer. "Nawl, she ain't bothering me.", I said. "Okay.", said Beverly. "Well, let me get some of this work off of my desk...I'm sure you got some catching up to do.", and when she said this, it was in such a flat way, that it kind of bothered me. "Yeah, you're right...I'll holla at you. Later Bev." "Okay Courtney.", said Beverly. Just as I was walking off, she looked back and smiled, and I smiled back, and went to my office bewildered. So ever since that episode, my friend Beverly has been distant with me. I call her and try to make conversation and all of a sudden, she's got something to do and she'll get back with me, but she never does. Unlike her! All this time, I'm working on finishing my book, because Beverly said if it's good, she's going to help me put it out, but her friends in her book club is going to read it also. So I've been going extra hard. I work on it at work, when I have time, and at home. I cut down on a lot of stuff

I do, just to finish this book, because in about a month, Beverly will have a book club ball. All black affair, and I'm going to be ready!

Beverly

Courtney had some nerve, talking to me! Oh I'm tripping! Courtney is my friend, I have no right being mad at him. Besides, I don't think he really knows how I feel about him. Yeah! I'm admitting to myself now. I've been feeling him, wanting him...bad!! But I didn't want to wreck a friend, in which I've found in him. He listens to me when I need to rant and rave, when I'm down and out. He's been a good friend since I've known him. Then too, the thing with me, I'm not going to be just some fling! I mean, a fling with him probably would be cool, but I really don't want to be just one of his women.. .one of his bitches. Nope! Not raised that way. Then on top of that, I heard him make a statement in the office the other day. I think one of the guys was telling Courtney about some guys who didn't like him, or was hating on him about some woman, etc. and Courtney hauled off and said "Long as my bitches love me!" Have you ever heard that song Lil Wayne, Future, and Drake got? Well, I feel like the "fuck them haters, long as my bitches love me" and when he said it, I was walking by, looking at him like "Boy!", and he smiled, and was like "Excuse me Beverly." Now it was vulgar. But it did something to me! I don't know, but ever since I've known him he talks like that. But... now, it does something to me, makes me hot! I don't know, I'm tripping. That night at the jazz club when Tisha told me that her and Courtney had exchanged numbers, I got jealous! But I couldn't be jealous because Courtney and I are only friends. But, about a week later, she called me and told me her and Courtney had already had sex. I called her a slut before I knew it. It was like, "Bev...guess what?" I'm like "What Tisha?" "Me and Courtney has already had sex! No...we fucked!" And before I knew it, I said, "You slut!", and she laughed and said "No you didn't?!" And I'm like "Yes I did! Tisha you don't just sleep with a man that fast. You got to get to know him and..." "I'm not trying to make him my man. Didn't you tell me after my divorce, I should just have fun? To go ahead and get me some?" I couldn't lie, cause I did tell her that. "Yes...I did..but.." "But what?", interrupted Tisha. I got quiet. "That's what I thought. Bev remember...I'm just having fun." So after that episode, I don't know why, but I kind of pulled away from her...again! A month passed since then, Tisha and I might have talked 2 or 3 times and she would let Courtney dominate the conversation. Courtney this, Courtney that, Courtney, Courtney, Courtney! And I would find a way to get off the phone with her. In fact, I was doing Courtney like that when he called. At work I would deal with him a little longer than on the phone, but I would try to get away from him. He was telling me how far he done got in his book, and that it would be ready way before the ball that my book club is having. He even came into my office and let me read the prologue, and it was hot! So hot, that it made me hot! My panties was moist when I got through reading it, and then it seems as if he knew it, because he comes right in with this smoky look in his eyes, like he wants to fuck me right there on my desk, and ask me did i like his prologue. I was stuck for a second too long looking in his eyes, but first looking below his waist. Trying to figure out the size of his dick! "Oh....my bad Courtney..I was...my mind was somewhere else.", I said and laughed it off. It seems to me that he's been picking up on my feelings toward him. Courtney would do little slick stuff. When we was tagging equipment the other day, he would kind of invade my personal space to ask or tell me something. "Excuse me" or "My bad". Like he knows I'm dripping for him, and I would tingle. I would try to give him space to let him know that I have retracted in my shell. He would pick up on it, but then I'll be mad when he gives me my space. Then extra mad because of how I'm feeling about him, and to top it off, what happened between him and Tisha!

Chapter 6

I've been in the lab like a mufucka! The lab, meaning in my room writing, getting this book together. Adding, taking away stuff, fine tuning. Beverly is on my mind lately. So much that it's bothering me. That way she's been in her shell. I've been trying to figure out what's wrong with her, but when I ask is she okay, she gives me this fake smile and responds, "I'm good.", and keeps on doing whatever she's doing. And that was getting to me because she is my friend! Then, I've been picking up on some other things from her. Things that are attracting me to her. Making me want to fuck her...bad. I can even go against my word and be her man. Her being so headstrong, independent, and fine is so attractive to me! To a lot of men, those qualities are intimidating, but not to me! I could be reading her wrong, but it seems as if she's trying to lure me to her. It's definitely some tension going on between us, but it seems like a lot of sexual tension. I don't want to take her the wrong way, but I think I'm right. Still fine tuning my book, as I listen to some music, and old time favorite song of mine comes on Jodeci, "I'll cry for you tonite." As I sit there and hit my Hennessy, my mind goes into overdrive. I'm reminiscing and shit, and I look at this picture I have from the company's Christmas party, with me and Beverly and a couple of coworkers, and I'm focused on my friend Beverly. That smile is what got me hooked. Damn let me snap out of it, and finish handling my business, because I'm taking this book to Beverly tonight. She can read it, run some copies and let her book club girlfriends read my book. After about 15 minutes of getting things together, I called Beverly. I hope it's not too late. It's 10:30 p.m. I was just about to hit the end button, and she answered, "Hello?" "Hey Bev! I don't mean to be calling you this late. You're not sleep are you?" "Ah..nope, but I'm headed that way.", said Beverly. "Oh my bad! I'll just wait till tomorrow." "No, what is it Courtney?" "I'm through with this book and...I know I could've waited, but I'm so excited. I wanted to know if I could bring this book to you? Just read a lil bit of it Bev? Or I'll just wait.." "Nawl, you can bring it now Courtney.", laughed Beverly. "Okay..okay, that's what's up. I'm on the way now!" I hung up, jumped up, and grabbed my car keys, the book, and hit the door.

Beverly

Now I don't know what Courtney is up to, but I'm going to be salty, in my shell, mask act back on as soon as he pulls up. How I'm feeling, I wanted to tell him that was very fucked up what he did! And yes, please come over here and make it up to me as if you owed me an apology, and let's have some make up sex. Oh my god! My mind is everywhere right about now. I really wasn't about to go to bed now anyway. I had done slept a few hours when I got out of church today, so my sleep is a little throwed off. All of a sudden, I'm self conscious about what I'm wearing. I got on a tank top and some black boy shorts! I don't want to send the wrong message, especially at this time of night. "Ma!" Is that Anthony hollering for me? "That's Courtney!", I said to myself. "Okay, I'm coming!" I ran around looking for something to cover myself up with. I reached and grabbed a robe, and it was short. Oh well. I put it on, and flew down the stairs quickly adjusting my attitude-mask.

Courtney

As I was driving over to Beverly's, I was going over in my mind how things had been going on between us in the past up until now. No hints of her wanting me, or me thinking that she wants me, up until recently. And she's most definitely showing it now. And I'm most definitely ready to get with it, with her. Right now! I'll just play it by ear. It's funny, but I'm getting butterflies the closer I get to Beverly's house. I shouldn't be like this, because me and Beverly have always been able to talk about almost anything. I guess the way she's been acting got me like this, but fuck it. I'll just have to deal with it, because I'm pulling up to her house now. I don't waste any time. I grab the book and jump out of the car, leave it running and jogged to her door and rung her door bell. Her son Anthony, came to the door. "Hey Anthony, how you doing?" "I'm doing alright." "Is your mother home?" "Yeah, she here. Hold on.", said Anthony as he hollered for his mother. "Mama! Somebody want you!" Then he hollered again. Then I heard her. "Okay..I'm coming!", said Beverly. Then she came to the door. "Wow!" is what I said to myself. Beverly had on some boy shorts, I think with a short blue robe with some type of designs in it, and a tank top. I know she caught my eyes, as I beamed down on those thighs right quick. The way she kind of closed her robe and cocked her head at me like "Boy!", trying to hide her smile. "Hey Courtney.", said Beverly as she took a deep breath. "Aye..what's up Bev?..Here's my manuscript...oh I mean my masterpiece!", I said,quickly getting in rare form, being me as I handed her the book. "Masterpiece.", said Beverly smiling the smile that she was trying to hold back. "Yeah! Wait till you read it.", I said, returning her smile. Can't help but to admire

Beverly in her at home look. The simple but sexy look is turning me on in a major way. She was feeling my vibe, because the look she was giving me made me know it. The look was saying, "I know what you want, but not right now!" Periodically rolling her eyes. "Okay Courtney. I'll see you tomorrow at work.", said Beverly bursting my bubble. "I'll read some of it tonight. I'll tell you what I think about it." Beverly seductively smiled, as she slid around her door like a cat. "Okay Beverly..see you in the morning.", I said as I hesitantly turned and slowly walked away. But before I walked away, I looked back, Beverly was looking at me as she hesitantly closed the door. And I caught her! "Bye!", laughed Beverly and closed the door. "Oh it's on! You can't fool me!", I said to myself walking to my car.

Beverly

"Ma are you alright?", asked Anthony, causing me to open my eyes. I was leaning against the door, clutching Courtney's book to my chest, breathing a sigh of relief, thinking "That was close!" I almost snatched him up in here, and told him how I really feel about him and Tisha and then take him right there in my living room. Up against the wall and .."Ma! Are you straight?" "Yeees.", I slowly said to my son, who was somewhat overprotective of me. "I am fine Anthony..you finished your homework?" Changing the subject quickly and walking to the stairs. "Yea ma." "Okay..I'm going to bed." I said and hurried off to my room to lay down and read this book.

Chapter 7

The week following the night I gave Beverly my book, Beverly was busy planning for her book club ball. She told me it was going to be an all black affair, with some masks, Mardi Gras type masks. Oh, and she loved my book! She read it in a day and a half! She's already made copies of it and let her book club members read it. I already had it copywritten, so I didn't have any worries about somebody stealing my material. I bought a ticket from Beverly, even though she invited me as a guest to speak on my book they've read or still reading. It didn't matter, Beverly was my friend, so I was down to support her cause. But I want to support another cause of hers, or should I say, support another need of hers. Some good loving! I already know Beverly doesn't have a man, and she don't do the sleeping around thing. Unless she's getting herself off, Beverly probably hasn't cummed in a minute. So, all the way up to this day, which is Saturday, the day of the ball, I had my radar instincts tuned up! I've been checking Beverly out all week in the office for signs and signals, but I've been analyzing them. I don't want to be wrong and read her the wrong way, but I think I'm on point!

Beverly wants me! While sitting here playing on the phone exploring different sites on the net, I get a call. It was Tisha! "Now I wonder what she wants!" I haven't been fucking with Tisha in some weeks. I wonder what she want. "What's up?", I said answering the phone., "What's up with you?", asked Tisha. "Shit..chillin, getting my car detailed. What's up with you?" "Just checking on you. I haven't heard from you in a while.", said Tisha. "Been busy.", I said. Trying to cut the conversation short or make it dry. "Oh..okay. I read your book! It was good!", said Tisha. "Thank you." "And why didn't you give me a copy first? I had to read it through Beverly. She gave me a copy." "Well Tisha, me and Beverly had already discussed.." "Yeah yeah.", interrupted Tisha. "I know y'all good friends. But are you coming to the ball tonight? I heard you supposed to do a lil speech. You promoting it already huh?" "Well..I guess you could call it that. But check this out, I think the guys are through with my car. Let me get back with you." "You ain't gone get back with me. So don't even say it. But wait till you see me tonight. You're going to want some of this pussy." "Ha ha!", I laughed. "We'll see.", I said. "Okay.", said Tisha. Then I hung up. True enough, Tisha had some good sex and dynamic head, but I can't keep messing with her young ass. After I paid the fellows for my car, I headed out to Decatur to holla at my cousin to get some kush. I'm getting straight to it tonight. Smoke me a nice cigarillo of some good marijuana. Down me a nice shot of some Patron Silver all before I leave the crib. When I get there, I'll be already feeling good, waiting to see what tonight brings. The night is set! I've bathed, put on my clothes, got myself together, now I'm in the mirror flexing. I got on my black emporio Armani pants, some black gators with suede trimmings from Fennix Italy, shoes black, Armani belt with a silver buckle, a black Armani long sleeves shirt with 3 buttons, a black brim on and some fly Armani glasses on! Yeah, I'm fresh! I smoked my weed earlier.

Half before I got in the shower, and the other half after I got out the shower, before I put my clothes on. I poured me a shot of Patron Silver. Downed it right quick. Popped a piece of Eclipse WinterFresh gum in my mouth and I was on my way. The Ball was held at the Cobb Galleria on Galleria Pkwy. So it didn't take me long to get there. As I pulled up, I noticed they had a nice crowd from seeing all the cars in the parking lot, and the line was out the door. As I was parking, my phone buzzed, and it was Beverly. "Hello?" "Um..are you planning on coming, or are you just being some type of star, and be fashionably late?", said Beverly. I laughed, "Yes I'm coming, and yes I'm being fashionably late." "Well Courtney, I hope you're not too fashionably late. Because in 5 minutes, they're about to call our names, and we're coming out to get this show on the road! You do remember that your name is getting announced, and you're coming out and making your lil speech?" "Relax baby! I'm here, getting out of the car now. I mean...Bev." I had done said baby before I knew it. "Okay, I'll meet you at the door.", said Beverly and hung up. Beverly seemed under pressure, she always have been the type to be very focused so that might be it. I don't know. I grabbed my cologne, "Chance Blue for men". Sprayed a little on and hopped out of my Beamer and headed to the entrance. Beverly was already there waiting when I got to the door. Damn she looking good with a short black skirt on, with one of her shoulders exposed, and some heels on. "Heey!", said Beverly as she hugged me. "Now come on!" Beverly grabbed my hand and led me through the crowd to the back hallways, by the dressing rooms, where her and her book club members were waiting for the event to start. "Here's the last piece of the puzzle right here girls.", said Beverly. All eyes was on me, like 2pac. Especially Tisha's. "Damn.", I said to myself. I forgot that she was a part of the book club. "Hey ladies, how are you all doing this evening?", I said. "Heey, how are you?", a couple of the ladies responded. "Um fine!", I said. "Sure is.", one of the ladies mumbled, and then came the laughter. I laughed also and played it off. By now, the weed and Patron Silver had done set in good, so I was feeling it like hell. "That book you wrote is good!", said one of the women. "Uh huh...made me hot!", said one of the women. More laughter, and then came the questions. But Beverly intervened. "Excuse me y'all. We have a table set up especially for Courtney, after they introduce us, after whoever is going to talk, including Courtney..okay?" "Okay, yeah you're right Beverly.", the women responded. "Everybody ready?", said a tall dark skinned balding guy. "Yeah...we're ready!", said Beverly. "Okay.", said the guy and disappeared. In a few seconds, he was on the mic. "Mic check..May I have everyone's attention. We are about to get this party started by announcing the members of the "Precious Jewels Book Club", and their special guest." The DJ was hyping the crowd up, and I was looking around the ladies of "Precious Jewels Book Club" as they was nervously gathering their bearings. I looked right at Tisha, who was already sneering at me. No doubt she was looking good with a very short dress on, but I wasn't going to fuck with her. I couldn't help it, but I kept looking at Beverly. God was she looking good, and I'm about to tell her. "Hey Bev." "Yes Courtney." "You're looking very, very nice tonight.", I said in a low tone, leaning in her ear she looked back and smiled. "Thank you. You don't look too bad yourself.", said Beverly and walked off. And I'm thinking, "What's up with her?". "Okay! He's about to call us out.", said Beverly. Yeah, that's what it is. This ball has her nervous. "The president of "Precious Jewels, the lovely Evette McKinely." Evette stepped out, strutted her stuff to "I like the way you move.", but Outkast. I think Beverly was next the way the girls was messing with her. She kind of looked back at me and rolled her eyes for whatever reason, I don't know. "Next up, we have the vice president of the "Precious Jewels", the lovely Beverly

Jackson." Beverly stepped out on "Queen of the night", by Whitney Houston. They had the doors open, to where we can watch as they came out. Beverly was really working it. Like she was on a catwalk for real! Then next was Tisha. She came out on "Get it Shawty", by Lloyd. After six or seven more women, I came out. I came out on "I'm Still Fly", by the BigTymers. Yeah, I was pimpin down the little walkway. Cool as fuck, swagged out, being me! I noticed a lot of women jocking me! Whispering to each other, smiling. I had noticed a lot of that from some of Beverly's book club members. After everything settled down, Beverly and her friend Evette did their thing. They had a lil thing for the people who was born in the 50's where they would dance. For the people born in the 60's and so on. They gave out some gift certificates. Now it was time for me to do my thing. At first, I was kind of nervous, but I already had it in my mind to make it short and sweet. The weed and alcohol had me slightly faded so I was good. "How y'all doing tonight?" "We ok! We good!", said the men and women who were mostly seated. "I would like to thank the beautiful ladies of "Precious Jewels" for having me as a guest tonight. And I'll like to thank you all, along with the "Precious Jewels", for supporting me by reading my book. Support a brother! Thank y'all!", I said and went back to my seat as they gave me a light applause. When I sat down, Beverly got up from her seat, turned her head towards me, covered her mouth and said, "You got some nerve.", and rolled her eyes and headed back to the podium to close out the speeches. "Huh?", I said astounded, because I'm trying to figure out what Beverly meant! After she closed out, it was time to party and do a mini book signing chit chat with the ladies and let the night take over. I was seated at the table talking to a few ladies about my book. I was getting all types of questions. "Are you married?" "Nope.", I answered. "For real?!", another woman asked. I laughed. "Is that hard to believe?", I asked. "Uh huh!", said a 3rd woman. "You never been closed to being married?" I laughed again, sipped my drink and said "Yeah." "I knew it!", said the first lady. I sat there and entertained these three over curious women, but at the same time I was looking for Beverly. I had a bone to pick with her. Lo and behold, there she was on, on the dance floor working it. With her lil fine ass! Now my attention is on the dance floor, watching Beverly dance in those heels and short skirt she was wearing. She must've felt me, because she looked right up into my face, as I was nodding my head, grooving to the beat. I smiled, she rolled her eyes. "That's it!", I thought to myself, as I turned my drink up and finished it. I'm going to get to the bottom of this. "Excuse me ladies. I got some business that deserves my attention.", I said, raising from my seat smiling. "Oh okay. We'll be here.", said the first lady who was flirting with me hard off the top. "Okay!", I said, barely paying them any attention, because Beverly is getting next to me in a major way, and I need to check my instincts. I headed to the dance floor, making my way to Beverly. She was dancing, doing "The Wobble". The DJ mixed the wobble song out and came with some Old School Luke, "Me So Horny"! They mixing it from old school, new school, back and forth. I approached Beverly from the side and tapped her shoulder, "Can I have this dance?" She looked at me and rolled her eyes, yet smiling. "Come on Courtney,", said Beverly. Me and Beverly was dancing quietly for a minute. Everytime she turned around, I would close in. But, it's like she has a sensor. She would step off, look back, roll her eyes, and turn around to face me. All I would do is smile at her. "What's wrong?" You okay?", I asked. "Yeah! Are you okay?", said Beverly. "Yeah..I'm okay. Look, if I offended you, I apologize!", I said. She rolled her eyes again, then she paused. "What you say?", asked Beverly. I guess she didn't hear me because the music was loud. I stepped in closer so she could hear me. She leaned her ear towards me. "Did I offend you?", I asked. Beverly hesitated and so "No!". Now I'm confused. But one thing I'm not confused about is Beverly nipples are hard right now! Harder than Japanese arithmetic. And she's turning me on, because it seems she's getting turned on and up for me. Her attention seems to be elsewhere, like she's preoccupied with something. "You know we always been able to talk.", I said, in an attempt to make her talk more. "I know.", said Beverly. She's about to make me do like Alpacino on "Scarface" when he was dancing with Michelle Phifer, and she was acting stuck up. And he stopped dancing with her and told her, "You got a look in your eyes, like you haven't been fucked in ages!" That's how I almost did. The fast music was fading out, and now they're putting on a slow jam. They were playing R. Kelly and Public Announcements "Slow Dance". Beverly was almost about to leave, until I stopped her. I reached out and grabbed her hand. "Now Beverly..you know I got to have me a slow dance." Reluctantly, she fell into my arms. "What's wrong?", I asked her immediately. "Nothing! Why do you keep asking me that?" "Because..the way you been acting. All distant with me like I done did something to you." Now I'm feeling this vibe me and her really have. The way she's breathing and looking. The way our bodies are responding to each other. I'm about to lose control! I'm trying to stop my dick from getting so hard. It's semi now. But this heat between me and Beverly is making it rise and throb into her. I know she feels it, the way she smirking. "No Courtney.", she breathes deeply. "I mean...". She's stuck, because now following my instincts, I done slid my hand down her waist, to her hips. "You mean what?", I asked. I can feel her getting lost in the moment, as I slowly grinded my hard dick into her. "I mean...you know...Courtney...I got to go!", said Beverly as she slid out of my arms. "Beverly! Hold up!". She stopped for a second, looked back and took off! I was right behind her, in a discreet way though. She was heading to the women's dressing room. She was casually stepping, yet quickly through the crowd. And I was casually stepping, yet quickly right with her through the crowd. "Hey where are you going?", said Tisha. She had done slid in front of me, bumping chest to chest. "Oh..what's up Tisha. I'm looking for somebody. But first I got to get to the restroom. Excuse me.", I said, trying to ease off. Beverly was still in my eye sight. Tisha just smiled. She watched me walk towards the men restroom. I looked back, that's when she turned her head, and I took advantage of that moment, and shot to the women's dressing room right behind Beverly. She looked back shocked. Putting her hand up to her chest. "Boy you scared me! What are you doing here?" "We need to talk! Now! Bev what's up with you? Keep it real with me now! I need to know what's been bugging you. We're way better than this!" Beverly stood there, looked at me, and smiled. Then she looked down, and when she looked back up, she had done wiped the smile off her face. "Courtney...you know what it is." "No...I don't know what it is. Tell me." Beverly squinted her eyes like, "You fool you!" And that's when she let me have it! "I can't believe you fucked her!! Oh my god! You really fucked her!! You slept with Tisha!", screamed Beverly, putting emphasis on slept. "Tisha's like my fucking niece, and you had sex with her!" "Damn Beverly, I apologize, but.... Tisha is grown. And what is the problem?", I asked Beverly. She is bugging on the fact that I had sex with Tisha when it shouldn't even be a topic of our conversation. It ain't like me and Beverly a couple, or fucking..we're just good friend, and she is acting the fuck up! "Yeah she's grown, but..but," "But what Beverly?", I asked. Wondering is my instinct on point, as I stand here, feeling the heat coming off of Beverly. Actually feeling two kinds of heat. The heat you feel, when someone (like your woman) is mad at you..and the other kind of heat, sexual! Unadulterated sexual heat! Sexual energy you feel when you and an attractive person is in a room together, and the both of you know that the obvious is on each other's mind, and the tension is so thick in the air, you can cut it with a knife! "What's up Beverly?" Still edging Beverly on, as I step a little closer, closing the gap, causing our distance to go from casual distance to intimate distance. And the temperature in the room rises. "I mean..what's wrong? Talk to me.", I said in a low tone. Voice getting husky because of the sexual tension and frustration I'm feeling. "What's really going on?" By this time, me and Beverly are face to face, which don't last but a couple of seconds because now we are both yielding to our unfulfilled desire, by attacking each other. " Mmm.", moans Beverly as our tongues touch. We deeply and hungrily kiss each other. Off top, I'm reaching up under this short skirt Beverly has on, gripping her ass with both hands and immediately pull her thong off and throw it on the counter. We're in the women's dressing room of the Cobb Galleria, where Beverly's book club is having an All Black Affair. "No.", moans Beverly, but is regular reaching for the button and zipper on my Emporio Armani pants. I help her by unloosening my belt and unbuttoning my pants and they fall to my ankles. I lifted her up on the counter as she wrapped her legs around my waist and penetrated her right there. "Sisss, oh shit!", I said as Beverly's twat gripped me like a vise grip, and I always wondered what her pussy hit like. And this is what I've been missing! After a couple of thrusts, Beverly all into it, threw her legs up on my shoulders, wrapped her legs around my neck, and went to throwing her pussy, like my dick was the last one on earth. At the same time, I snatched her to the edge of the counter, hands cuffing her shoulders and went to standing up in her. Meeting her thrusts halfway perfect timing. "The door.", said Beverly. "It's locked.", I said, quickly alleviating her fears of anyone catching us. Especially Johnny, her ex husband. Even though they are divorced, he still half way checks up on her. So he was there to support her book club event. I locked the door as soon as we stepped in the dressing room. Both of us must been on the same page, because we sped up to make this a quickie, a well performed quickie. I didn't want this to look funny, both of us exiting the women's dressing room together, and I'm sure she didn't either. But I do want to do more with Beverly, like get her to a bed. I'm damn near on some lovemaking, all night shit right here. "Oh Lord!", said Beverly as she's about to cum. "Harder!", moans Beverly and I do just that! Bang her harder, like I'm auditioning for a porno flick. Within seconds, we both explode! I'm about to collapse on top of Beverly as she slowly slid down the counter top, on my dick, and it hasn't even softened up yet, after I nutted. I slowly stroke up into Beverly, as I roughly lift her back up on the counter. As I speed up and stroke a little harder, I'm getting turned on by watching my dick go in and out of Beverly dripping coochie, and now, I'm instantly rock hard, all the way up! It's like watching a triple XXX black film when there's a close up scene, and the couple is meeting each other halfway, meat to meat. "W-w-wait, wait, hold it, hold up. Siss, ooh shit, hold it!", a gasping and panting Beverly said. "What's up?", I asked. "Look, look Courtney. Let's go...let's go to my place.", whispered Beverly as I pulled my hard, shiny dick up out of her and let her off the counter. She grabbed her thongs and put them on, and I pulled up my boxers and pants, and we quietly, but quickly exited the dressing room. Beverly eased and got her purse and coat, knowing that someone was going to stop her and talk. And they were going to wonder where she was going. I grabbed my coat, and quietly eased out the door, thinking the coast was clear, and there's Tisha, standing at my car. "Fuck!", I mumbled to myself, as I stepped in the parking lot. Not breaking a stride, as I walk to my 645 BMW. I don't feel like messing around with Tisha. Especially not now. Beverly went ape shit on me once she found out I had sex with Tisha, and now me and Beverly done fucked. How sparks just flew between me and Beverly,

I can't let Tisha hinder me from getting it in with Beverly tonight. We got to finish what we started. So now I'm thinking, how am I going to shake Tisha? Quick thinking before Beverly comes outside to her car.. "Hey Tisha what's up?" "Hey Courtney. Now where would you be going this early, when our book club is honoring you?" "What the fuck?!", is what I'm thinking to myself, because she is right. But one thing about it, I've already given my little speech and kicked it with the lovely ladies of the book club. "Oh Tisha...feel like I'm coming down with something. A stomach virus or something.", I said, hoping that would kind of brush her off. By this time, Beverly came out the door, heading to her car, but looking my way the whole time. "Look Tisha, I really need to be moving on." "Oooh, I get it.", said Tisha, as she was following my eyes, where I looked toward Beverly. "Get what?", I asked. "You and Beverly are leaving! What y'all hooking up or something?", asked Tisha looking back and forth at me and Beverly as she is getting in her car. I messed around and seen one of those beautiful thighs as she was getting in the car. "You trippin!", is what I told Tisha as I got in my car. "Nawl, you are trippin! Don't be mad cause you're busted!", said Tisha. "Busted?", I said, slightly irritated. "I tell you what..I'll holla at you.", is what I told Tisha as I was pulling off. "Damn! She think she my woman!" All I was thinking about was catching up with Beverly. She had already pulled off, so now I'm riding breaking the speed limit. I kept thinking about our episode in the dressing room and was trying to get Beverly to have round two. I showed up at Beverly's house just in the nick of time, because she just getting out of the car. She paused for a second when I was pulling up and headed to the door. I didn't know how she was going to act about Tisha being at my car at the ball. But, I held my composure as I walked up behind her and she was unlocking her door. I leaned down and kissed her on her bare shoulder, and she kind of leaned away. Now I'm confused. "What's wrong?", I asked Beverly. "What was Tisha talking about?", asked Beverly. "Being nosey. Asked me where I was going, and said that me and you was hooking up. Being messy." I leaned in for a kiss, and she kind of leaned away again, but still let me kiss her lips. "Bev there's nothing there okay?" "Is she going to be a problem?...I mean..don't worry about it.", said Beverly as she opened the door. We walked in the house and hung our coats up. In mid step, Beverly turned around to face me with tears in her eyes. "Courtney...I don't want to be hurt." Now that touched me! "Bev, I'll never hurt you. I value our friendship..I value." "It's past that now.", said Beverly, cutting me off. I was kind of speechless now. All I could do now was hug her and hold her. Then all of a sudden she giggled. "What?", I asked. "I'm trippin.", said Beverly and wrapped her arms around my neck, looked me in my eyes and slowly we kissed. At first, I was back up under her skirt, squeezing and caressing her butt. The skirt was short, so it had done rose up and that made me hot. I was taking off my shirt, and she was helping me as she caressed my chest, causing me to quiver from her touch and anticipation. We quickly was undressing right there in the living room. "Hold it.", said Beverly. "The bedroom.", and she looked down at my dick as it was pointing out of my boxers ready to strike. That made me hug her, as she turned around. We walked to her bedroom just like that. Me behind her, holding her, dick throbbing up on her ass, and I'm reaching around slowly digging in her panties, making her super wet. "Ooo Courtney!", moaned Beverly, as we made it to her bedroom. As soon as we crossed the threshold, she was pulling her thongs off with my help. Beverly turned around and was helping me out of my boxers. I reached down with my left arm and grabbed her right leg. She wrapped it around my waist, as I picked her up. She wrapped the other one around my waist and to the bed I went. Beverly was grabbing my dick, guiding me into her. I put my hand behind her knees, right in the bend, and pent her legs to the bed. Knees up by her ears! I got up on my tiptoes and went to work on Beverly. I got it in like that for a little while, till my toes started to hurt and then I laid on in. Grabbing her by her ankles , getting my pound game on. Letting her ankles go, I grabbed the bottom of her head board for leverage, and balled up on Beverly like an ant when it is biting. Omg! This woman's love box is so good, while I'm hitting it, my mouth started to water. I let the headboard go, yet making it bang against the wall, I started sucking on her calf muscle, as I brought her knees together, to her forehead. Still got her legs up high and poked us into a frenzy style climax. "Ouch!", softly said Beverly as she giggled. "What are you doing?" I was still biting on Beverly. "Trying to see what flavor you are." Is what I told Beverly. I let her legs down and started kissing her. Damn! I can't get enough of this woman. Beverly was enjoying herself because she has a sparkle in her eyes. "What?", asked Beverly. Because I'm just looking in her eyes. "What's on your mind?", answering a question with a question. She takes a deep breath, closes her eyes, smacks her lips, opens her eyes, and slowly answers. "Where...are...we now?" "In your bed.", I answered, and kissed her. She frowns and punches me in the chest. "Not funny!" I roll off Beverly, to my back. Now she's leaning over me, elbow planted by my ear. "I'm waiting.", said Beverly. Now..me and Beverly been friends and coworkers for about 2 ½ years. Yes, it had crossed my mind on getting with Beverly on several occasions. But, I knew that Beverly was a good girl, who might've not put up with me at the time. Yes, I love good girls, but I was having way too much fun at the time being a bachelor. She knew I was a dog. So, I spared her and decided to just be her friend. When I was in a relationship, she gave me sound advice and when she was going through her divorce or was having problem with men, family, etc. I was there for her. I must admit, this is very awkward. "Umm...are you deaf?", asked Beverly, snapping me out of my thoughts. "Oh no Bev...just thinking." "Okay..so are you going to answer me?" "Yeah...where do you want this to go?" Another question with a question. "Courtney!..You know me..you know how I am." "Yes I do..that's why I asked you...where do you want this to go?" Beverly just rolled her eyes and let out a breath of exasperation and fell head first on my chest. "Uggh!" "It's gone be alright. We'll figure it out.", I said, as I ran my fingers through Beverly's hair. "Yeah, we'll just let things flow.", said Beverly. All the time we're laying there, the radio is playing softly and I paid attention to what was on. "Hooow do I address you? Heey lover, hi friend. How you doing, where you been?", sings Mary J. Blige. Beverly and I both feel the lyrics to this song at the same time. We look at each other for a moment, both knowing that this must be a sign!

(To Be Continued)

Frank and Tracy
Chapter 1 Feb. 2017

It was one of those cold, boring nights, a Friday night at that. Sitting around the house, with nothing to do besides watch t.v., Frank decided that he would get up, and get out and about. Grabbing his keys off the dresser, he notices a ticket to a play. "Damn! Where this come from?", Frank asks himself. It dawns on him, as he reads the ticket. "Oh Todhs gave me this ticket." Tosha was Frank's cousin. Tosha would've went to the play, but something came up, so she called Frank. "Hey cuz, what's up?", said Tosha. "Just cooling cuz, what's up with you?", said Frank. "I'm okay cuz..but look, I got these tickets to this play by Mahdi Theatre Company, but I'm not going to be able to go. Something came up. So I was wondering did you want to come by and get them? You know, take somebody out on a date or something." "Umm..okay, I'll come by and get one.", said Frank. Stressing the word one. Tosha was always trying to get Frank to go out on dates, ever since his break up with Samantha. It seems Frank was going through something after the break up. So Tosha was trying to make sure that he was okay. "Cuz, I got two! I know you can find one of your lady friends who will go." "Nawl, I'm good cuz. I'll be by there to get the ticket.", said Frank. Right now Frank wasn't interested in the dating scene. Maybe a little, but not heavy at the moment. Catch him a female he probably used to date, or just hang in a cougars den and get chose and later get attacked in bed by some horny fine lonely, but older chick, who loves younger men. Frank didn't have any problems getting women. He was tall, athletic, and handsome. And he was definitely about his money! Frank ran his own sports management/agency and drove a fly ride. A Monarch blue cL65 AMG Mercedes Benz, a nice two story bachelor pad, and dibble and tabs in the real estate game successfully. Ladies choice. Frank drove over to the theatre by himself to check it out. "What the hell!", Frank said. "Ain't shit else to do!" As he arrived, pulling into the parking lot, Frank noticed that there was a nice crowd. Particularly a lot of women. "Damn!", said Frank under this breath. As he was trying to find a parking spot, two fine ass women in tight skirts, dressed and heels walked in front of his car. "Damn. Might have been a good idea to come to this play after all.", said Frank to himself as he parked his car. It didn't take Frank long to get inside and find his seat. After he left the concession area, buying a soda, as he approached, he noticed this jazzy, caramel complexion, lioness, sitting in the seat next to his. Lioness, not really in the animalistic sense, but in the aspect of her felicity. She's sitting there with "I know I'm the shit!", radiating off of her. To go along with the cute round face feline-like qualities in her features, makes her desirable or at least get to know her. Frank is thinking this to himself as he approaches his seat. She noticed Frank's startled look as soon as he looked at her. But she kind of brushed it off. "Excuse me?", said Frank. "Is anyone sitting here?" The brown beauty looked up and smiled. "No..I mean as long as I've been sitting here, no one has. Your seat number should be on your ticket stub." Frank looked down at his stub. "Yah...that's what I was looking at..I'm at the right one.", said Frank as he sat down. "Actually..I thought someone might've been sitting next to you and probably stepped off for a second.", said Frank. Making small talk, but getting to the business on sly. "Uh..no..no one was here." "So this pretty ass woman here by herself, with no date?", Frank thinks to himself, sitting there, contemplating for a couple of seconds, should he keep the conversation going? Yes! "Look, I don't mean no harm, but...what I really was saying is..you don't have a date? Or you chose to come see this play by yourself?" The beauty looks down at her lap and smiles, as if she is choosing her words carefully. "Um, well.." "Hold it..my bad!", said Frank motioning with his hands apologetically. "I didn't mean to make you feel uncomfortable or nothing." "No, you're okay..you good.", laughs the beauty. "My name's Frank.", said Frank. "Okay..my name is Tracey." They hesitantly shook hands. "Like I said, I didn't mean nothing, I just thought maybe your husband or boyfriend might've been sitting here." That struck a nerve with Tracey, due to the fact that Lewis doesn't do things like this with jer. But she masked it, and sugar coated it. "Nawl..he didn't wanna come. He had a lot of work to do.", said Tracey shifting in her seat because she's lying. Lewis doesn't go out with her much and things were going downhill with her and Lewis. So she did stuff like go out by herself, to get away from him and to get his attention. Either Lewis was slow or he just didn't care. Tracey actually was wondering what a dude was at a play by himself. Not wanting to probe too much and Frank was a total stranger to her. So, she didn't want to have to give too much information. Just to get information, but she couldn't help herself. "I'll be careful.", Tracey said to herself. "So..Frank. Why are you here by yourself? Where's your wife or girlfriend?", said Tracey, stressing the wife and girlfriend. Not trying to seem too flirty and send the wrong message, but she couldn't help it. Because Frank was attractive. Frank laughed. "Girlfriend, wife? I have neither one. I'm single. My cousin, she gave me a ticket to this play. Well, she tried to give me two tickets, thinking it would be a good idea for me to take a date..but nah. I'll check it out by myself." This kind of made Tracey curious. "I don't think he's gay.", Tracey thought to herself. Maybe he's fresh out of relationship. To confirm Tracey's curiosity, Frank said, "Well actually Tracey, I'm fresh out of a relationship. So...that's why I'm by myself.", said Frank, nodding his head assuringly. "You know, just getting my head together." "Ohh!", said Tracey nodding her head smiling. "I understand." Before she knew it, she had done put her hand on Frank's forearm. "Oops! Sorry.", said Tracey snatching her hand back. Frank just smiled. "You're cool.", said Frank, making her get back in her comfort zone. Frank began to ask questions about the play. "You know anything about the new actress, the chick who's playing the main female character in the play? Joyce Richardson?" "Well..not really. I had seen her once, on this BET sitcom.", and the conversation carried on all through the play, at a whisper, they talked. That night after the play, Frank and Tracey exchanged numbers, and became very good friends. Platonic friends. Platonic friends with the magnetism of curiosity, drawing them toward falling for their unfulfilled desires.

Chapter 2 Feb. 2018 1 yr. Later

Frank and Tracey's relationship had blossomed! They shared almost everything. Frank was still living a bachelor's life. He had done got back on the dating scene playing the field. Just had women who were cut friends. Friend with benefits, fuck friends. Still wasn't looking for no girlfriend. No feelings was involved in the way he ran his game. The only woman he had feelings for was Tracey, and it was unconditional love. They both were attracted to each other, but they kept all of that in control. Tracey had revealed to Frank that her relationship with Lewis was really on the rocks, but she was still trying to work it out with him. So Frank just chilled, and waited his turn. He knew Tracey was a good girl, bout his business and sexy as hell. Independent, professional black woman, what he wanted, but he didn't press. He just remained her friend. They met up at least 2 or 3 times per week. They might have lunch or dinner, or she would just go by his place and chill..without nothing happening. Earlier in their friendship, he had tried Tracey once, to see what was what. It was maybe a week or two after they met. They was talking on the phone one night, she couldn't sleep. Frank had been drinking a little bit, and he already harbored some sexual attraction towards Tracey, and it just came out that night. "Tracey, I don't mean no harm, but...you already know I find you attractive and...why don't you come over? Let's talk about it?" "Um..Frank, you okay?", said Tracey. "Yes..I'm okay..why you ask me that?" "I'm trying to stay true to form, and you're trying to make me misbehave!", laughed Tracey. "Well, I'm only trying to help.", said Frank. "Look..just be my friend right now Frank.. You can handle that can't you?" "Yeah..I can handle that." After that night, Frank didn't try her again. Normally, Frank would've backed up a little, maybe even lost her number, but he had a genuine like for Tracey. He wanted to be her friend, have her back, and hold her down like a man was supposed to. So he decided to be her friend, but still have desire for her, but not letting it show too much and regularly. She knew it, but she still dealt with Frank, as long as he respected her mind. Frank was patient, but at the same time, had enough sense not to put his life on hold for her. He did his thing with other women, and Tracey knew it and respected it. They were there for each other when one needed an ear to listen, or a shoulder to lean on. They even had keys to each other's home. Well, Frank had a key to Tracey's duck off spot. Her private retreat on Flagler's Beach, when she wants to get away or she needs her creative juices flowing. This was the first place she bought when she got her first paid commission job. A party for the 16 year old daughter of a local senator. It was the place she picked out with her father before he died. Their special place to relax and enjoy life. Her mother had left them when she was a little girl. Tracey had a few issues like everyone, but she was ideal and special to Frank. For one, it was sexy when a tough woman wanted you or potentially wanted you, but don't need you. Tracey had it going on financially also. She was an event planner for 12 years for FAMU'S event center, and owned a few residential real estate she was renting out. She left FAMU, and branched out into her own business as an event planner-coordinator. Tracey has a large building that can hold up to 2,000 people. She has a fully functional kitchen staff of 20 (1 manager, 2 chefs, 5 prep cooks, 8 waitresses, and 4 waiters. The manager oversees the kitchen with the head chef and she also books all the events. Her name is Jessica. Tracey only really works on the coordinating of other people's parties, because she likes the field work. Meeting the people, and putting their thoughts into something beautiful and unique. So to Frank, Tracey was everything he ever wanted in a woman. How it would be to making love to Tracey every other night. Waking up behind her, all on that lil fat booty she got. Giving it to her early in the morning, and just chilling around the house all day. It was going down soon. Frank felt it. Confirmation of the fact that Tracey and her man, Lewis's relationship was about to end..soon. Tracey had called Frank, letting him know what was going on. Confirming his instincts. "Hello.", grudgingly said Frank. "I'm sorry Frank!", laughed Tracey. "I woke you up, I know!" "Yea..you did that.", laughed Frank as he looked at the clock on the nightstand. It was 3 in the morning. "You alright?", asked Frank. "Well...I will be.", answered Tracey. "I just found out some more disturbing stuff on this dude Lewis. And I'm getting tired. And then he got the nerve to cop an attitude, when I confronted him." "That nigga hit you?", asked Frank sitting up in his bed, "What's up?" "No, no, no.", said Tracey. "What I told you about that? He knows better!" "I'm just saying Tracey. You sound upset, then it's 3 in the morning. What happened?!" "Frank, you know I can barely sleep anyway, and this episode ain't make it no better. I just need to talk. It can wait. I'll wait until the morning when you wake up." "Nawl, I'm up now.", said Frank. It was a Saturday morning. Frank didn't have any work to do until later on that night. He had to meet a client in Miami. "It's cool. Now what's on yo mind?" "Okay...you know I have let him get away with a lot of bullshit..right?" "Yea.", said Frank. "Then this chick that go to our church, I found out they had been texting each other. Not too long ago, it was this chick he went to college with. You remember I was telling you about that?", said Tracey. Tracey went on about that, telling Frank the situation. "And now,to top all of this off, I think he's been ducking Brenda's daughter, which I took on as my god daughter." "Nooo!', said Frank. "He denies it, but I think he did. It came out that he had been calling her..regular!" "How did you find that out?", asked Frank,and Tracey began telling him about it. "And the lil wench had the nerve not to tell me! She was like, "He's been calling me. I just didn't tell you because I didn't want to make you mad." That's what she said. After all that I've done for her.`, said Tracey, as her voice quivered. "I found out that he had called her and asked her would she like for him to cook for her." "Oh yeah?", said Frank. "Yeah!", hollered Tracey, getting emotional. "That's not it..he even asked her once to come over and get some drinks. Can you believe this bullshit this fool is trying to pull off?", screamed Tracey. "Damn.", said Frank. By now Tracey was in tears. "I'm sorry Frank.", sniffed Tracey. "Nawl you cool Tracey, get it out.", said Frank. "I can't believe it Frank! And he already is lacking with me. He's lacking affection. He don't love me. He's lacking bed. Yeah I said it. We barely have sex." As Tracey was ranting and raving, Frank was thinking how he could fulfill all the needs that Tracey wasn't getting fulfilled. It would be easy for Frank, because he already adored Tracey. And she already basically told him everything, so, he was well on point. After that morning, for about a week straight, Tracey and Frank talked a lot. On the phone, meeting up in little low key bars. The mall. Frank was just being a good friend Tracey needed. Tracey enjoyed her business, but at times it got a little stressful, but she handled that. What added on to her situation was a surprise she never was prepared for...Anticipated, but had little faith in..her mother popped back up in her life!

Chapter 3

Tracy & Momma

On a sunny, summer morning, 4th of July of 1981, to be exact, 8 year old Tracey woke up to hear her mother and father arguing. "Elaine, it's just so much I can keep tolerating! I mean...you must think that I'm some type of doormat! You stay out all times of night..doing..God only knows what!" "I was at my sisters house!", screamed Elaine. "You're lying! You need to come up with another one.", said Doc, Tracey's father. "The reason I know you're lying is because I came over to your sister's house! You weren't there Elaine!" Tracey's mother was looking stunned, for a second. Then her eyes turned to slits. "So Doc....what are you doing? Stalking me now? What..you don't trust me Doc?" "Prove that you can be trusted Elaine!" Hollered Doc. that statement stopped Elaine dead in her tracks. She slowly turned around and looked at Doc, as she was headed to the kitchen, to pour her a drink. "So, that's how you feel Doc?", said Elaine as she poured her some Gin. "Yeah Elaine..that's exactly how I feel. And you need to put that down. You've probably been drinking all night.", said Doc, as he reached for Elaine's glass. She snatched away, almost spilling it. "I'm grown!", said Elaine. "Well act like it!", yelled Doc. "You know what Doc?..I'm out of here! Fuck this shit!", said Elaine as she went to the bedroom closet, grabbed her suitcase and commenced to packing her clothes. Tracey had been listening from her bedroom door, with tears in her eyes. She didn't know what to do, or whose side to take. She loved her mother, but she was always a daddy's girl. Tracey was very smart for an 8 year old, so she knew her mother was in the wrong for staying out all the time. She had watched her father suffer quietly from all of this. She could tell her father had not went to the bedroom where her mother was. That;s when she made the decision to go find her father to see what was going on. She opened the door, and walked down the hall to the living room to find her father sitting on the couch with his hand on his head, and eyes closed. "Daddy..are you okay?", asked Tracey. Walking up to her father, ready to comfort him. "Yes baby..I'm okay.", said Doc as he held out his hands receiving Tracey in his embrace. That's when Elaine came out with her bags and suitcases and car keys in hand, and stopped dead in her tracks when she saw Doc hugging her daughter. Tracey turned around when she heard her mother. "Momma, where are you going?", asked Tracey. Elaine stood there looking at her daughter with tears in her eyes, which in turn, made Tracey's eyes tear up. "Come here baby, and let mama explain to you.", said Elaine as she sat her suitcases down. Tracey ran to her mother as she sat her suitcases down. Tracey ran to her mother as she sat her suitcases down, and hugged her. "Momma don't go! Please don't leave me and daddy!" That made the tears flow down Elaine's cheeks. "Baby..I got to. You can come with momma Tracey." "No! I don't want to be with just one of y'all! I want both of y'all!", screamed Tracey. That's when Elaine looked at Doc who was still sitting on the couch, rubbing his temples. "Elaine..don't make your daughter do this.", said Doc. "Do what? You're the one who is making her choose!", screamed Elaine, as she rose up from hugging Tracey. "Me? I'm the reason Elaine?" And from there, they were arguing back and forth. "Mommy. Daddy, please stop it!", screamed Tracey, putting her hands over her ears. Tracey walked up to her father hugging him. That's when Elaine snatched her luggage off of the floor. "Tracey..you coming with momma or you going to stay with yo daddy?", said Elaine. Tracey was crying looking up at her daddy. "Daddy..what are you.." Elaine didn't let her finish. "It looks like you succeeded turning my own daughter against me! Because it looks to me she's chosen a side!" That's when she turned on her heels and walked towards the door. "Mommy!', screamed Tracey. Elaine stopped at the door for a second or two. And walked out out of the door, without looking back. "Mommy!", screamed Tracey and ran to the door. By that time, Elaine was getting in the car. Tracey opened the door and went on the porch. Elaine was cranking up and putting the car in drive. But just before she pulled off, she looked at her daughter standing on the porch, crying with Doc standing behind her. Doc walked down the steps. "Elaine!", said Doc. she waved at Tracey, mean mugged Doc, and pulled off. "Mommy!", screamed Tracey as she cried, and Doc walked back on the porch and hugged his daughter. That was 35 years ago, and that was the last time Tracey had seen her mother.

Chapter 4   2018

It was such an emotional time for Tracey, now that her mother had popped back up, in her life. " I can't believe it Frank!" "Just like that!", said Tracy snapping her fingers. " After all these years, she pops back up in my life... unbelievable!", said Tracey, as she turned up her long-island tea. Frank was sitting across from Tracey, nursing his drink, being the forever attentive friend, that she had found in him. It was through facebook how Elaine reconnected with her daughter Tracey, through a friend request. As soon as she had got it, she called Fank. " Frank, are you up?" ,said Tracey. "Yeah... I'm up now..", laughed Frank, as he raised up in his bed with his phone to his ear. " You alright?", groggingly asked Frank. "I'm Sorry Frank. For waking you up, but you got to listen to this!" Please hear me out for three minutes, okay Frank?", laughed Tracey. " I'm okay.. But then I'm not!", said Tracey. "You listening?", nervously said Tracey. " Yeah, I hear you." , laughed Frank. "Guess who sent me a friend request on Facebook?" "Who?" "My Mother!", hissed Tracey. "Out of all the people...my momma, who ran out on me and my father thirty-five years ago!! We didn't know whether she was alive or not! Well... We heard she was, but she never contacted us!" "So what did you do?" Did you confirm her request?", asked Frank. "Uh... Yes.", said Tracey. " So... did you send her a message? "Uuh...no! But she sent me one.", said Tracey. "Ookay.", slowly said Frank, edging Tracey on. "So what did she say?" "I'm sorry!.", answered Tracey. "That's what she had the nerve to say. I'm Sorry!!! After all these years! I'm Sorry." "Ok Tracey... Calm down. Did you respond?" asked Frank. "Why I sure didn't.", said Tracy as she went on to rant and rave for five strong minutes explaining her reason for not responding. "Well look. We're going to hook up later on and discuss this over a drink or two, is that cool with you?", said Frank, "Okay... That's cool Frank.", giggled Tracey. "I'm sorry for waking you up with this, but i just had to talk to somebody about this! "You cool," said Frank. Later on, they hooked up at Applebee's and discussed the matter over drinks after they ate. "Unbelievable Frank, and then when I went through her pictures, she has a lot of pics of me when I was little, up until the point of now!" "Yeah... and you look just like her!", laughed Frank as he pulled the pic back up in his phone. Tracy had sent him a picture of her mother, in which she had downloaded from Facebook. "Yeah, that's what they say.", said Tracey. " So Frank, what do you think I should do?" "What you mean?" "I mean... I mean, about the whole situation in general! Should I send her a message back? And if I do send her a message back, should I accept her apology? And if I accept her apology, should I just do it using only a couple of words, like "You're forgiven" or " I forgive You" and just leave it like that? I don't know, it's just so much I want to say to her. I want to let her know how I felt, as an eight year old girl watching her mother leave. I want to let her know how I've been feeling about her the thirty-five years in between that time, eight to forty-three years old," said Tracey, as Frank handed her some napkins to dry her eyes. "Thanks.", said Tracey as she wiped her eyes. "I'm sorry Frank, for taking you through all this, but thanks for being here for me.", said Tracey, at the same time touching Frank's arm. "You good with me Tracy, you know I got your back." "I know.", smiled Tracey, "unlike somebody else I know! Somebody that should have my back, but don't.", Tracey was speaking on her boyfriend Lewis, who's been slacking in their relationship. " Speaking of him, where is he now?" asked Frank. "I don't know, he supposed to be in Mobile, Gulf-Shores, somewhere up that way. But you still haven't told me Frank, what you think I should do about this situation with my momma?" "Oh yeah," said Frank. "Tracey... I know this a touchy situation for you...but... this is your mother, and I know that you're probably mad at her for leaving you. I can only imagine what you went through as a child and what you must be feeling now...but... keepin it one hundred with you. I think you should go ahead and send her a reply on Facebook, exchange numbers, and get to know yo mama! I mean... in my opinion and a high percentage of people in the U.S.A, along with me, would feel that your mother was wrong for leaving you. If she wanted to leave your father, cool, but if she could've taken care of you, you should've been with her! But... with all that being said, I think you should kick it with your mother, yeah. Let her know how you feel, but go ahead and give her a chance. We only have one momma." Tracey was quietly shedding tears, taking in what Frank was telling her. Frank handed her some more napkins. "Thanks.", said Tracey, and then she got up from the table. "I'll be back." "You okay?", asked Frank. "Yes.", smiled Tracey, "Just heading to the ladies room to get myself together." Tracey was thinking about what Frank had said. It made sense. She had so many questions for her mother as well as so much anger she wanted to unleash on her also. " Oh well, I might as well go ahead and send her a reply," said Tracey, as she went to Facebook on her phone and sent her mother a message. "You are forgiven... and here's my number (850-763-9112). "There.", said Tracey, "See where this goes!" Tracey gave herself another look over in the mirror and went back to join Frank. She barely made it back to the table and her phone alerted her to a text. "Damn, that was fast.", said Tracey looking at her phone. "What?", asked Frank. Tracy turned the screen of her phone towards Frank, so he could read the text. " Hi... This is Elaine." "Wow! That was fast.", said Frank, after he read the text. Tracey told Frank about how she responded to her mother on Facebook, forgave her, and inboxed her number and now she was just sitting there looking at her phone. "You're going to text her back or what?", asked Frank. "I mean we know it's going to open up a whole new world, but... fuck it! It's going to have to be done Tracey." "I knooow.", said Tracey, as she leaned forward. They both was quiet and Frank raised his eyebrows and opening his hands as to say "Well." "Okay Frank.", said Tracey, as she text her mother back. "Hi... it's been a long time...mother." "Look Frank.", said Tracey as she showed her reply text to her mother. "Is that good enough? I mean... I don't want to sound too mean, or sarcastic, but..what am I supposed to say to her? She's a total stranger to me! She didn't even attend my daddy's funeral.", said Tracey. "Okay Tracey..calm down, calm down!" Frank gave Tracey some more napkins to wipe her eyes. "Look.", said Frank, placing his hands on Tracy's free hand. "I know this is hard for you, but know that I'm here. I got your back." That one comforting gesture made Tracey smile through her tears, and put some already existing thoughts of Frank's, into full throttle. "Damn! He's so caring. I want to just dive over this table into his arms.", thought Tracey to herself. "Thanks Frank.", said Tracey with a smile. "I don't know what I would do without you." With that being said, Frank and Tracey were both quiet staring each other down. Tracey's phone vibrated, breaking the silence and tension between them. "It's Lewis.", said Tracey looking at her phone. "Hello?", answered Tracey. As Tracey listened to Lewis, Frank ws finishing off his drink and checking his phone at the same time. "Whatever Lewis! You can take as much time as you need up there! Me? Attitude? Nah, not really. Whatever!", said Tracey to the phone and hung up. Tracey laid her phone down and closed her eyes as she rubbed her temple. "You okay?", asked Frank. "Yeah, I'll be okay. Let's go!" Frank paid the tab, and they walked to the parking lot to racey's blue M6 BMW. "Thanks again Frank, and don't worry about me. I'll be okay." "You sure?" "Yeah.". Smile Tracey. Then she hugged Frank and surprisingly, he smoothly planted a kiss on her jaw. "Be easy Tracey.", said Frank as he swaggered off to his Mercedes, leaving Tracey smiling with her eye kind of bucked in amazement. Still watching Frank as he got in his car, that's when she suddenly remembered she was supposed to be getting in her car. "Lord what am I going to do? What am I going to do?", said Tracey to the empty car. And that's when Frank pulled in front of her car. "Text or call me when you make it home safely. Aight?", said Frank as he was slowly pulling off still looking at Tracey for a couple of seconds, and she was returning his gaze. "Frank..you just don't know!", said Tracey as her panties got moist and her clit throbbed. But little did she know, Frank did know, or thought he knew and was saying the same thing as he pulled off. "Tracey..you just don't know!", as pre cum was at the tip of his dick as it throbbed.

Chapter 5

A couple of weeks had done passed since Tracey's mother had done came back into her life. That night after they texted each other, they had been talking. Tracey even invited her over to her house, which was something she had to think about. She had talked to a couple of her girlfriends about it. Her crew. The three T's. Tracey, Tanita, and Talissa. "Giiirl!! That shouldn't be too hard of a decision to make.", said Talissa, who's one of her most closest friend. Her ride or die chick. "I mean..I understand how she just left you and your father and all...and all those years, you were hurting..but you done forgave her..right?", asked Talisa. Tracey closed her eyes and took a deep breath before answering. "Yes." "Okay then..just be nice to her, and invite her over, and y'all just vibe. Get to know each other.", said Talissa as she reached over and touched Tracey's hand,comforting her friend. "I think she's right.", said Tanita, nodding in agreement. "Okay.", said Tracey. "It's just..this is opening up a whole new world.", said Tracey. "We knooow!", said Tanita and Talissa in unison. "But it's got to be done.", said Talissa. "At least it needs to be done.", said Tanita. "That's the same thing Frank said.", said Tracey. That's when it seemed like the music stopped. All eyes were on Tracey. "Whaat?", said Tracey with a startled look on her face. Talissa rolled her eyes at Tracey, as Tanita looked at them and started laughing. "Whaat?!", asked Tracey again. "Chile please.", said Talissa as she laughed. "Giirl, when is you going to go ahead and snatch that man?!", asked Talissa, "You know he wants you! And you want him! Speaking of me...umm..what's up with Lewis?", asked Tanita. "Nothing!", said Tracey. "Nothing at all! And oh..on the subject of Frank. We're just good friends!", smiled Tracey. Letting Talissa know she caught and heard her comment she made about Frank. "Friends?! With the very high potential of a friendship-flourishing into an intense romance.", said Tiffany, using her hands, stressing flourishing. Being dramatic, "Na-na, nawl!", smiled Tracey, closing her eyes, picturing her and Frank being a couple. Then picturing her and Frank fucking each other. "Yeah right!", said Tanita. "Look at her. She's blushing now!", laughed Tanita. "It's written all over your face.", sang Talissa, mimicking the old men at large song. "Why don't y'all stop playing with each other Tracey, and get it crackin?", said Tanita. "He does have your back. He has a strong interest in you. In a caring way. And it's obvious y'all are attracted to each other. I can just feel it when I'm around you two!" They all laughed and discussed the situation. Meanwhile, Frank was just closing out the last meeting at his sports management office when he got a text from Angela. Angela was a chick Frank had met at a club and had been messing around with on occasions. Nothing serious. But sex here and there. No strings attached. A fuck thing. He was contemplating not responding to Angela. But then too, he didn't want to have her salty with him. Who knows, he might have to make a booty call soon with Angela. So, with that in mind, he texted Angela back, with a "Just kooln. How are you?" Once Frank texted Angela back, he called Tracey to see what was up with her. It was by routine. He would call her as soon as he was about to close up his office for the day to see what she was up to. Even though they be done already talked a couple of times throughout the day. "Hello?", said Tracey. "Heey!", said Frank. "Heey Frank!", said Tracet singing his name as to let her friends know that he was on the phone. "Heey Frank!", said Tanita and Talissa. In which made all of them giggle. "Wow! What a reception? What did I do to deserve a greeting like that?", laughed Frank. "Oh Frank, you didn't do nothing. We just kidding around. Actually we were just talking about you over a couple of drinks.", said Talissa, leaning into Tracey's ear so Frank could hear her. "Talking about me? What happened?", asked Frank, sounding surprised. "Nothing! Stop it Lisa!", laughed Tracey as she playfully hit Talissa on the arm. "Talissa got jokes Frank! So what are you up to?", said Tracey trying to change the subject. "Just about to leave this office. What you got going on?" "Oh, we just sitting around, having a few drinks, talking.", said Tracey. "And yes, you are the topic of our conversation.", said Talissa. Tracey leaned back into the couch, looking at Talissa frowning, because she's kind of getting irritated now. And in response to Tracey's displeasure, Talissa put her hands on her hips. Tracey got up from the couch. "Be cool would you Lisa?", said Tracey, as she walked off. Tanita was laughing on the low. "Damn! What was that all about?", asked Frank. "She just tripping. Done got tipsy.", said Tracey. "Ooh.", said Frank. Tracey could tell he wasn't buying her response. "Okay Frank. Yes, we was talking about you. At least they were. I just was responding." "Ha ha.", laughed Frank. "Okay..what was it about me?" A slight pause. "Okay Frank.", said Tracey, and she told Frank about the conversation. "And that was it.", said Tracey. "Hmm.", said Frank. "Huh?! What does "hmm" mean?" "Just thinking Tracey. But check this out. I'm about to go get me something to eat. You hungry?", Frank was good at changing the subject, and Tracey knew it. "Matter of fact, I am. What are you having?" "I don't know. I might stop by Burger King or Wendy's.", said Frank. "Yeah. Do Wendy's. Get me a salad, and some chicken nuggets, and a sprite." "Got ya.", said Frank. After they hung up, Frank was thinking about what Tracey told him about their conversation about him, and he was doing an assessment of it. Drank was thinking about how they became friends. Their friendship started from him trying to get with Tracey. But they agreed to be friends upon Tracey's wishes. Now things were really on the rocks between Tracey and Lewis. And Tracey and Frank's chemistry was off the chain! "I wonder do Tracey see this like me and her friends do?", said Frank to the interior of his Benz. frank respected and loved Tracey platonically, but from the very first time he saw Tracey, he was attracted to her, wanting to do more than just fuck her. He damn near possesses her. He wanted to be her man. With that thought in mind, Frank hurried to Wendy's to get him and Tracey some food. He was ready to be in her presence, with the irons what was currently in the fire, heating things up.

Meanwhile, Tracey, Tanita, and Talissa sat around and had a few more drinks and was chit chatting when Frank rang the doorbell. "Heey Frank.", said Tracey in her flirtatious way. "Heey Tracey!" said Frank, smiling at Tracey as he handed her her food. "Thank you F rank.", said Tracey receiving her food. "Are you busy? Wanna come in for a minute?" Frank hesitated for a second because he didn't like to be in her house, knowing that Lewis could pop up anytime. Then, in Frank's eyes, it was disrespectful. "Nawl Tracey..I'm cool..then too, you know I don't rock like that.", said Frank. Tracey paused for a second and slowly smiled. By that time, Talissa walked up. "Heey Frank!", said Talissa. "What's up Talissa!" "Um..where's my food?" "Oh my bad! I knew I should've.." "No Frank, I'm just kidding!", said

Talissa, "But what I'm not going to kid you about is my friend here."
"Talissa!", said Tracey. "Talissa nothing! Look Frank..you and my sister
here need to stop playing. Y'all need to go ahead and make it happen."
All that time Tanita had done walked up laughing. "Heey Frank!"
said Tanita. "Hey Tanita." "Is Talissa up here harassing you?" "Nawl
she aight.", said Frank smiling at the whole scene. Because he could
tell they had been drinking, and all they had been talking about or
whatever's on their mind, is liable to come out. "Come on girl.", said
Tanita, grabbing Talissa by the arm. "Let's let them talk." "Remember
what I said Frank! You too Tracey!", said Talissa as she was being led
away. "That girl is crazy!", said Tracey laughing. "Well look..I guess I'll
be running along now. You okay?", asked Frank. "Yeah I'm okay. Are
you okay?", said Tracey. "Yeah I'm good." They stood there and shared
an awkward silence. "Whaat?", said Tracey. It's nothing..I'll call you
when I get home.", said Frank as he began to walk off. "Frank what's
up?", asked Tracey. "I'm cool. I'll call you.", said Frank. "So Frank,
you're doing me like that?" "Haha!", laughed Frank. "Doing you like
what?" Tracey put her hands on her hips and cocked her head to the
side. "Come on Frank! You know we read each other." "Oh really?!",
laughed Frank as he was about to walk off. "Yeah!.. Really.",flirted
Tracey. "You be easy baby.", said Frank as he walked on to his car.
"Hmm, okay..you do the same Frank..call me!", said Tracey. By now
Frank was at his car. "You gone be up?", asked Frank. "Yeah..they'll
be gone in a minute.", said Tracey. Frank paused as if he was about to
say something. What he wanted to ask her was Lewis coming home
tonught, and if not, fuck calling. He could chill with her. But instead,
Frank chilled. "Okay Tracey..I'll do that. Take it easy." "I will Frank.",
said Trcey as she seductively stepped back in the house, and slowly
closed the door. As she watched Frank, with knowing eyes, he returned
the look. Tracey's knowing that Frank wants to take her inside and get

into some steamy sex. After about an hour from leaving Tracey, Frank called Tracey and they talked till the sun came up.

Chapter 6

"Get the fuck out of my house Lewis!", screamed Tracey. "Tracey! What I.." "No! Now Lewis!", said Tracey cutting Lewis off. "Pack yo shit, and get out of my house! I'm going to leave. I'm going to give you an hour..and when I come back, you and all your belongings need to be gone." "Wait..Tracey baby let me talk to you! Let me explain..come here!" "No! Fuck that!!"m said Tracey as she walked to the kitchen, went in the refrigerator, grabbed a gallon of water and went back upstairs to the guest room, where she left her goddaughter, Olympia. Knocked out, naked on the floor, Tracey poured the gallon of water on her to wake her up. Tracey had knocked Olympia out, when she came home and caught her and Lewis in the guest room having sex. When Tracey came home, she felt something was wrong when she seen Olympia's car parked on the street, a little past Tracey's house headed to her neighbors house. She would've missed it, if she wouldn't have cancelled her meeting and if she would've came her regular route. That's coming from the regular way in which she would've reached her driveway first, but instead, she came into her neighborhood the back way in which she approached her neighbors house to the right of her house first. When Tracey was pulling up, noticing Olympia's car parked there, immediately aroused her suspicion. She kept going, driving past her house, to her neighbors house, 2 doors down, and turned around and parked. Aware of the fact that her neighbors or anybody who recognizes the silver Lexus GL 450-SUV, they're going to wonder a little about her truck being down there. Tracey didn't care, she was following her female intuition. Tracey took off her heels, and grabbed a pair of Nike running shoes that she conveniently keeps in her truck in case she gets the urge to go walking or running. It was getting dark, so she had great coverage to run to her neighbors fence and jump it. She would be right in her backyard. Tracey was very athletic, so it wasn't a biggie to jump the fence pretty fast. Once she got in her backyard, she swiftly ran to the back door, unlocked it, and slid in. The house was dark, and quiet, minus some slow music she heard playing upstairs. "I know the fuck they're not!", Tracey mumbled to herself as she took the stairs two a time lightly. Once she got on the landing, the music got a little louder, and so did the unmistakable ..sex groans and moans! "Sisss, ooo baby! Suck it with yo fine ass!", moaned Lewis. Tracey couldn't believe her ears as she stood there at the guest room door stunned. Tracey was sure the door was locked, but she grabbed the knob anyway to make sure. To her surprise, it was unlocked! She slowly cracked the door, restraining herself from just busting in the room, and going the fuck off. The music was getting louder as she cracked the door a little more. It was ironic that the song on was Dru Hill's classic, "Someone is sleeping in myyyy bed!", crooned Sisco through the surround sound. Tracey had done slipped in the room unnoticed, at the time Lewis was slowly taking his dick out of Olympia's mouth and changing positions. "Bend that young ass over baby!", said Lewis. "Yeah and you love this young ass don't you?!", said Olympia as she grabbed Lewis's tool and guided it in her from the back. Just as Lewis got one or two pumps in, Olympia opened her eyes to look into Tracey's eyes. Tracey stood there for a second with tears streaming down her face and instantly went at the sweaty couple. "Aaaww!", screamed Olympia at the same time. "What the fuck!?", screamed Lewis startled as he looked back to see why Olympia was screaming, and he was cumming at the same time. This really made Tracey go ape shit! She kicked Lewis in the ass and caught him with a right hook square in the mouth, busting his lip. "Auggh! Tracey! Stop!", hollered Lewis grabbing his bloody lips. That's when Olympia quickly grabbed her clothes and tried to dart for the door, but she was a little too slow. Because Tracey had done snatched her by her hair and punched her hard in the face, knocking her out. "Bitch!", hissed Tracey as she spit in Olympia's face and walked off. "Tracey wait!", screamed Lewis. Tracey kept walking and went straight to her bedroom closet to her gun case, where all the guns her daddy had left her were. Lewis, kind of aware of where she might be going, took off behind her, to the bedroom and grabbed her. "Wait Tracey! Don't do it baby, I'm sorry!" "Let me gooo!", screamed Tracey as she bucked her head back against Lewis's nose, nearly cracking it. That caused him to drop her, because now he was grabbing her nose. That's when Tracey went downstairs and Lewis followed.

After pouring the gallon of water on Olympia, she awoke startled. "Get yo clothes on, and get yo lil slutty ass up out of my house! Remember what I said Lewis! When I get back, both of y'all need to be gone!" After Tracey said that, she stormed off. When she got to her truck, she got behind the wheel, put her head down, and cried. She cried for about 2 minutes straight. Once she got herself together, she sat there for only a brief minute, and then she crunk up and pulled off. The first person she called was Talisa, Talissa's phone went straight to voicemail. Then she called Tanita, and Tanita wasn't answering. "Damn! Where are all of my friends when I need them?", said Tracey. That's when she thought about Frank. She went to his name in her contacts, and called him. It wasn't late, so she knew he was up. Probably was at his office. He didn't answer, and this really pissed Tracey off. That's until her phone rung within seconds after she hung up...and it was Frank. "Heey, what's up?", said Frank, in that deep baritone voice in which Tracey loved and found calming. "Hello! Tracey? You there?" "Yeah..yeah..I'm sorry Frank..I'm here.", said Tracey trying to get herself together. His voice did something to her instantly. A calming effect and to go along with that, Tracey's mind instantly goes into overdrive. Thinking how would it feel to be picked up and carried to her bed in those muscular arms of Frank. "What's up? You're okay?", asked Frank as he was walking to his car. Tracey took a deep breath before answering. "Yes and no Frank! Frank..I caught that son of a bitch fucking Olympia in my house!", said Tracey. That statement stopped Frank in his tracks, "Noooo!", said Frank. "Yees!", said Tracey, and she commenced to telling Frank what happened. "Frank...are you still there? Hello?", said Tracey after she got through telling Frank what happened. He was so quiet on the other end as if he was stunned. "Yeah Tracey..I'm here.", said Frank. What was going on in Frank's head was that he already peeped what was going on, or what was about to be going on when Tracey had told him a while back about the situation. He never spoke on it when Tracey used to tell him about it, keeping it player. "Oh Frank, I just don't know what I'm going to do!", said Tracey. "What you mean you don't know what you're going to do? Tracey you're stronger than that. The first thing you're going to do right now is meet me at B-Sharpe Jazz Cafe in 20 minutes. You think you can do that?" "Yeah." "Okay do that Tracey. Nawl, matter of fact, I'm going to talk to you till we meet up." "Okay Frank." Frank knew that Tracey wanted to go the fuc off, so he figured if he could get her somewhere that's peaceful, he could calm her down. Frank talked to Tracey the full 20 minutes it took to get to B-Sharpe's. Trying his best to comfort her, and that's Tracey loved about Frank. He was genuinely caring. Once they arrived at B-Sharpe, pulling in at the same time, they parked next to each other. They looked at each other and smiled. Frank got out of the car and went to Tracey's passenger door and climbed in. "You aight?", asked Frank. Tracey smiled as she wiped her tears with a napkin. "Yeah, I'm okay..but they need to be gone from my house! Seriously Frank!", said Tracey as her lips quivered and tears began to roll down her cheeks once again. You could tell that she had been crying. Frank leaned over and hugged Tracey. "It'll be okay,", said Frank. "Just let it on out." Tracey let the Levee's break and flood with tears. "Let it out.", said Frank softly like he was soothing a child. Tracey cried for a minute or two and Frank held her the whole time. "I'm sorry Frank. I done cried all over your shirt.", laughed Tracey. "You straight..come on, let's go in the club and sit down and talk. I'll buy you a drink.", said Frank. "Okay.", said Tracey and they got out of Tracey's truck and walked in B-sharpe.

After an hour of talking, and having two or three drinks, Tracey had calmed down. She had turned her phone off after Lewi kept blowing her up. She was through with all the talking. All she wanted was for him to be done packed his clothes and moved out. "Come on Frank, I'm ready to go. I don't mean to be holding you up. You might have something to do.", said Tracey rising from her seat, and grabbing her purse. "You okay?", asked Frank as he got up from his seat. "Yeah..I'll be okay. I'm going to Talissa, and get her to meet me at my house.", said Tracey as she turned on her phone and hit speed dial, ignoring the texts and missed calls from Lewis. "Talissa? Girl let me tell you what happened.", said Tracey as she began to tell her friend what happened. When they made it to her truck, Tracey discontinued the call. "Talissa let me call you back." "No! Girl you are going to stay on this phone with me until you meet me at your house! I'm on my way." "I'm good Talissa. I'm on my way. Let me talk to Frank.", laughed Tracey. "Frank?!", said Talissa. "Ummm, uhh! What..he's there with you? Now?? At a time like this?! Girl you should be getting you some right now!" "Now, now, hold up ma'am! Let's not get too far ahead of ourselves.", said Tracey. "Whaaat?!", screamed Talissa. "Bye girl! I'll call you right back said Tracey and hung up. "Wow! What was that all about?", asked Frank. "Talissa tripping.", laughed Tracey. Not wanting to tell Frank what Talissa actually said because it was true. "Frank, thanks for being there for me." "Anytime. Do you need me to follow you home or something? I mean...is you straight?" "Yeah, yeah. I'm good Frank." "Are you in shape to drive?", asked Frank. "Yeah I'm okay. Thanks Frank.", smiled Tracey. "I'm still going to follow you home." Tracey stood in the door of her truck with her hand on her left hip, smiling, warming and tingling all over for the fact that Frank really do care about her. "Okay Frank, I'm not going to argue." When Tracey arrived at her house, her friends Talissa and Tanita were there waiting. Lewis and Olympia were gone. "Hey ladies. How y'all doing tonight?", said Frank from the window of his Benz. "We're doing okay.", said Tanita. "How are you?", said Talissa. "I'm good.", said Frank. Tracey walked over to Frank's car and thanked him once again. "You're welcome Tracey. Call me if you need me.", said Frank. "Okay Frank..I'll call you later.", said Tracey and walked over to her friends and Frank pulled off.

Chapter 7

After Tracey put Lewis out, her and Frank got a little tighter. Frank had started going to her house off and on, for a friendly visit. Tracey had a rule about inviting men to her house and that rule was not to do it, point blank. But with Frank...she was feeling Frank and Frank was feeling her, even though they wasn't a couple, nor were they having sex. They had almost a romantic friendship, and they had each other's back. As Trcey;s going through drama with Lewis and Olympia, to go with Tracey's long lost mother popping back up in her life things were very hectic for Tracey. Tracey's mother had started showing up on a regular needing money. Tracey gave her mother the benefit of the doubt. One, this was her mother. Even though she left her. Two, she could be down on her luck just for the moment. But the more she showed up, which was more regular, she seemed to look worse, appearance wise. To top it all off, she had nowhere to live. So now, the evidence of addiction was peeping it's ugly head out in her mother's action. She had asked Frank what was his take on the situation. "It don't sound good to me Tracey. I mean...when she came to town, she was living in a hotel until she got her own place?" "Right.", said Tracey. "Which has been 70 days to be exact!" "Okay.", said Frank. And then they went all over the details again. "She smoking.", said Frank. "Smoking? Smoking..like crack or something?", asked a bewildered Tracey. "Yeah..wonder how I know huh?" said Frank. "My pops was on it. So I know a lot of the symptoms and Tracey, your mother sounds like she's displaying a lot of traits. "Now she needs a place to stay.", said Tracey. Frank was quiet for a moment before he answered. "Tracey..that's yo momma. You gotta take her in. Just pay attention to her. Then you can go from there." Tracey sat there staring in space. "Yeah you right.", said Tracey. When Tracey's mother moved in, everything was okay..at first. It wasn't long until stuff had started coming up missing. The first thing Tracey recognized was missing was some imported silver. Tracey had asked Elaine had she seen the silverware, and Elaine played dumb. "Baby, I don't know nothing about no silverware. Where was it?", said Elaine. "In the pantry.", said

Tracey pointing towards the kitchen. "Don't worry about it.", said Tracey as she walked off from her mother. Tracey grabbed her phone and walked outside and called Frank and asked him for his advice. "Call every pawn shop in the city Tracey. Call them first." And that's what Tracey fif. At first, it seemed as if she was searching for a needle in a haystack after the 10th call. Then she got lucky on the 11th pawn shop. The owner told Tracey to come down to the pawn shop. Tracey went to the pawn shop and the owner showed her the silverware and video surveillance. "Oh my god!", said Tracey shaking her head, as she watched the film of her mother passing the silverware.. "Ma'am, do you know that lady?", asked the pawn shop owner. "Yes, that lady is my mother." "I'm sorry ma'am." "It's okay. What does she owe you?", asked Tracey. The owner told her what he paid for it, which was way lower than it was worth. Tracey paid for the silverware and left. Soon as she got in her truck, she called Frank and told him what happened. "I'm sorry to hear that Tracey.", said Frank. "So what are you going to do?", asked Frank. "I'm going to confront her, get to the bottom of this, and offer her some help if she has a problem. Because she's not going to be able to stay with me and steal from me.", said Tracey. "I'm headed home, I'll call you later Frank." Tracey hung up the phone and sped home.

"Mama..it was you I was looking at on that surveillance camera at the pawn shop..pawning my silverware!" "So blame yo mama huh?!", said Elaine as she sipped her liquor. "Just like yo daddy!", hissed Elaine. Tracey could tell her mother had been drinking a little heavy, opposed to how she presented herself when she first popped back up into her life. When Elaine first came back, she wasn't drinking or nothing and said she hadn't had a drink in 5 years. Tracey had heard that she liked to drink and was kind of wild back in the days, but Tracey didn't know about Elaine's addiction to crack. Stunned by Elaine's comment, about Tracey's daddy, Tracey said, "Look...daddy don't have anything to do with this." "Okay...if calling it how I see it, is "Just like my daddy, then so be it! Yeah...a shovel is a shovel, and a spade is a spade. That;s what my daddy told me." Elaine was kind of startled by Tracey's statement, but she didn't say anything. She just looked at her for a couple of strong seconds and she turned around and headed to the door. And at that moment, Tracey's mind flashed back to when she was 8 years old when her mother walked out on her and her father. "Yeah..go ahead and leave just like you did 35 years ago! That's what you're good at. Running away!", said Tracey. With that being said, Elaine stopped at the door. Stunned. She acted as if she was about to say something...but she didn't. She just twisted the door knob, and walked right out the door, and Tracey slid down the wall, while crying out for her mother, like she did when she was 8 years old.

Chapter 8

"Tracey! Open the door!", said Frank. Tracey had called Frank and told him what happened, and when they talked, she sounded very faint, so he told her he was on his way. When he got to her house, she wouldn't answer the door. After he rung the doorbell a couple of times, and she knew he was on his way, so he found that storage. Especially after he had called her again while he was at the door. So now he was banging on the door and hollering her name. "Tracey!!" Still no answer. Frank went around to the backyard and tried the backdoor and to his surprise it was unlocked. "Tracey!!", hollered Frank. Frank went through the whole bottom level of the house and then ran up the stairs. "What the...?? Tracey!!" He found Tracey sitting on the floor against the wall, head down as if she was knocked out. He kneeled down in front of her and that's when he seen the empty bottle of liquor sitting on her side. "Tracey! Tracey!", said Frank as he gently slapped her face. "Oww.", said Tracey responding to Frank's slaps. "Woman...are you okay?!" She looked up at Frank and smiled. "Fraank!", slurred Tracey. You could tell she was drunk.

Frank made sure Tracey was okay. He really wanted to take her to the hospital. "Are you okay? You want to go to the emergency room?" "Nooo!", laughed Tracey. "Just help me to my room." She tried to stand up, but the alcohol had her. Frank scooped her up, and took her to her room and laid her down on her bed. Frank grabbe a trash can and sat it by the side of the bed, just in case she threw up. "You want some water Tracey?" She just nodded and Frank went to her lil personal refrigerator in her room and got a bottled water. By the time he made it back to Tracey, she was asleep. Frank sat the water down on her nightstand, searched her closet and found a blanket and laid it across her. Frank, being the type of guy that he was, wasn't interested in taking advantage of a drunk woman, so Tracey was safe. What he did do though was kiss on her forehead and quietly left.

Chapter 9

Tracey's mother had not returned since that night she had left, nor had she heard from her. Swallowing her pride, after about the second week, she dialed her mother phone number to only find it to be turned off. Her friends, Tanita and Talissa, were by her side, but she spent much of her time talking to Frank. She had so much compounded stress on her. And her plate was so full. Tracey hopped in her truck and drove off to her getaway. Once she arrived at her spot, she sat her purse down, and sat on the couch. She grabbed the remote and turned on some music. She sat there with so much on her mind. She had to figure out so much with so little time to make it all happen. She thought Lewis had her back but when everything was said and done, she was all alone with her problems, and then some. She leaned back and closed her eyes, grateful that she had her apartment to herself. This was her getaway, a place to call her own. She had always been independent and she was really grateful for that now. Only one other person had her key. Her dear friend and he was out of town building up his business. They met about 2 years ago, and they instantly became friends. He was a good listener and she was grateful to have him in her life. She didn't know what to do about her pressing issues, although some would call them minor, she was overwhelmed. She felt herself drifting away and she felt she was not alone but she was extremely tired so she remained in her reclined state. She awoke to a touch and the smoldering look in Franks eyes. Eh said he was worried about her and came back. He asked her to lay in his arms and told her things would be okay. As she lay her head on his chest, the tension began to leave. She began to feel a new kind of desire. It was as if her body was speaking another language that only he could understand. She dozed off and this began the fantasy. She dreamed she was being held and caressed until every muscle in her body was relaxed, but suddenly, she felt a burning inferno inside. She had a fire that needed to be quenched and at that very moment, his hands brushed her inner thigh. He had long since told her that he was a thigh man, so this was a very enticing move for her to experience. Unknowingly, she let out a moan of desire. He had been watching her as she slept wondering what had her moaning so seductively. He knew he should wake her, but the moans were making him feel things, intimate things and he wanted to carry out the act of fulfilling them with her. Now how was he going to tell her this and maybe ruin their friendship. What if she didn't feel the same? Just as he was thinking these thoughts, she rubbed her hands in his chest and called out his name. He looked at her carefully, and realized she was still asleep. He wondered again what was making her moan and why on earth was she calling his name? He wanted to kiss her lips and touch her body in places that were well covered. She stretched again, and her hands fell down to his lap, brushing his private parts. He had to clinch to keep from reacting to his most primitive desire. He decided he would watch her a little longer to see if she said anything else. She was going deeper and deeper into her fantasy. He had now gone from her inner thigh to her abdomen and his caresses were getting deeper, the pressure was just right and she felt the moisture between her legs. She moaned again, but louder and her hips moved putting her lower body almost in his lap. He lost a little control and placed feather like brushes up and down her arm. She moaned a little more and he moved his hand down to her leg. He was so nervous, so he just laid his hands palm down on her thigh. Now to her this was starting to register, but only in her fantasy world. She was so intoxicated with his smell and the pressure of his hand that she didn't know her moans and movements were triggering him to go to a place he had long dreamed of going. He started to caress her thigh and decided he just had to touch her hot spots. He placed his hand at the juncture of her thigh and felt the heat. She moaned and moved even closer which allowed him to get even closer. The moaning is soon followed by the slow sensual movement of her hips. He applied a little more pressure feeling the heat and wetness of her inner core come through the silkiness of her panties through the shorts that she wore. He knew that if she didn't wake soon and stop him, he would want her so bad that he would say and do what he had to in order to consummate this process. His words and actions would be heartfelt, but he had been trying to keep that to himself for the sake of their friendship. He truly valued their relationship and did not want to jeopardize it by having sex. Her body enticed him and he wanted her. He had always wanted her, but when they met she was involved with another man, that he knew was not right for her. So he decided to become her friend and wait it out, but he refused to let her get too serious with that chump because he wanted her for himself. Finally, that fool messed up and it was over. Now was the time! He knew she had some other things going on, but he just wanted to be there for her. He leaned over and brushed his lips against her temple. Then he kissed her eyes. He just couldn't resist her lips. They felt so soft. He meant to only brush his lips across hers, but just as their lips touched, she parted her lips and let out a soft moan that sent chills through his body, down to his very soul. He put more pressure on her lips and she returned the kiss. As the kiss deepened, she opened her eyes. At first she was totally surprised, but it felt so good, she just couldn't stop. He was the first to pull back. She looked at him and asked, "What just happened?" His reply was, "Nature." She smiled at the witness of his answer, but she needed more. So she asked again, "What are we doing?" He had a quick comeback, but knew she wouldn't take much playing around, so he answered her in earnest. "I have desires for you and nature just happened. You were lying here and you were having some kind of dream which triggered my reactions, and led to that kiss." She giggled because she was thinking about the dream, and thought to herself, if only he knew. Then she said oh what the heck and told him that the dream was about him. He smiled and was very happy to know he was the cause of all her moans. He asked her if he could officially kiss her and she said yes. He looked at her closely, and lowered his head to experience this much awaited act. The kiss was slow and sensual at first but ended up being steamy and hot. He felt like he was about to explode, but he knew he had to keep it together. She pulled back and asked if she could get closer. Now he was thinking she couldn't be any closer unless she sat in his lap. Which is just what she did. She took that sexy body and straddled him and leaned in and really kissed him. When she pulled back, he asked her if she was really trying to make him lose control. She laughed and asked if that was possible. He just looked at her. Tracey was very adventurous, so she decided at that very moment that she would see how far she could push. She wiggled her hips and watched his eyes grow smoky. She felt the pressure of his dick and that caused her to get even wetter. She realized that his decision to pressure him could cause her problems. She realized too late, because he grabbed her hips and held her firmly so she could really feel the pressure of his member and know exactly what he wanted to do. He reached up and pulled her head down, and kissed her passionately, letting his feelings flow from him through her. She had long since wondered if he could fulfill her needs but since they were friends and she was with Lewis, she had never dwelled on the thought much. She was smiling and he was watching her. He pulled back just a little to ask her what she was smiling about because this smile had a different edge to it. She told him she was wondering something and had a question to ask him. Hoping he would not take it the wrong way, and not wanting to appear to brazen she forged ahead. She looked down at him and asked, "How much are you working with?" Now he was totally confused, so he asked what she was talking about. She had never done anything like this before, so she was really unsure as to how to ask the question. She decided to try to explain. She started out with, "Once upon a time I would often dream that a man would come along and just sweep me off of my feet, and when it came to love making, he would touch my very core; so I need to know if you can enter me and touch my core, but you got to have enough to do that. So what are you working with?" Now he was starting to get the picture, but he wanted her to say exactly what was on her mind, so he said, "What do you mean touch your core?" She was getting frustrated, and he could tell, so he told her to just say what was on her and don't try to make it sound so intelligent. He wanted her to make it to the street. He felt that she had this inner person in her that was raw, street, hood, and he wanted that person to come out, so he could her "rough love" could be good love. She leaned back a little, but he would not release the hold he had on her hips, because he loved the way she fit into him, and he loved the warmth of her body as it met him. The feel of heat and wetness on his dick was almost too much but he needed her to say what she wanted before he could move forward. She took a deep breath, and asked, "Do you know how many inches you are?" He said, "Yes. I am 6 feet inches, do you want me to calculate that in total inches or does that answer your question?" Now that was not what she was talking about and he knew it, but he was going to get her to say the words if it was the last thing he did, but the last thing he wanted to do before sleeping was fuck her. She looked away, but he told her to look at him and he would help her say the words. He asked what she wanted and she said "I want you.", and he said now say what this is, pointing down to his dick. "A penis." He told her to say the street name, and she looked at him and with a little encouragement, she said, "Dick!" Now, he told her to put it all in a sentence. So she said, "I want you, and I want your dick, but I need to know if it can fill me." He said, "Well, I think 10 inches should be enough, but if not, then I know what and how to do what I need to do so you can be satisfied."

She directed him to take his shirt off. After that, she started kissing on his neck, licking it slowly. She reached down and grabbed his dick and started stroking it. She moved down, and started sucking on his chest, going from nipple to nipple. She was about to drive him crazy. He lifted her and put her on the couch. He removed his pants and boxers and picked her up and placed her on the floor on the plush carpet. He parted her beautiful thighs with his legs and rammed his dick up in her. He started drilling and grinding hard, but she was meeting him stroke for stroke. Their rhythm was in sync. He deeply kissed her as they were reaching their climax, hard and fast. Round and round she met him, she used her muscles to grip him, milk him, making him lose his breath. He emptied in her as she moaned his name, which signaled her climax. They remained in that position for a moment, him still inside of her. He kissed her passionately and as she returned his kiss, he felt himself growing hard again. She was moaning with pleasure and this was totally turning him on. He was thinking about all of the positions he wanted to put her in, but right now he just wanted to enjoy the deep stroking;long, hard, and deep. Realizing this was a much awaited dream come true and as he pushed harder and deeper, he continued the kiss. He pulled back and looked into her eyes, seeing the fire in her eyes did things to him as he climaxed again, and he felt her climax with him. He laid on her for a minute to catch his breath. He rolled over to his side, but he took her with him and as they lay on their sides looking at each other, they fell asleep. Such good love making..

Chapter 10

.They laid like this asleep for what seemed like hours, but in reality
was only 45 minutes. He was holding her so tight that when she
moved in her sleep, she brushed against him, and with that movement,
he was awakened. He looked at her as she slept and brushed his hand
down the side of her face. Now this simple movement awakened her.
She looked at him and smiled. He brushed the tip of her left nipple
which sent chills down her spine. She could not believe it, but she
really wanted him and she was growing so hot, her clit was throbbing!
It was almost unbearable, she wanted him to touch her down there
so bad! Even though they had done all the things they had done, she
was still a little shy. She had never done any of the things she had
fantasized about in real life. She wondered what he would think about
her if he knew some of her fantasies. She was afraid to even think
about it because she felt that was not normal. But right now, she just
wanted to enjoy his company, and she really, really wanted him to
touch her body completely. He looked at her and told her that the next
lovemaking session should be in the bedroom, so he stood and reached

out his hands for her. She took his hand and slowly followed him to the bedroom. He stopped short of the bedroom door and turned to look at her. He needed to tell her that if she wanted to stop she could and he would understand. He knew that once they walked through the bedroom door he could not let her go nor could he share her with Lewis. He wanted her mind, body, and soul completely. He needed her in his life to complete him to make him feel whole. He told her all this while they were standing and she could not imagine not walking through the door with him and experiencing all that he had to offer. Not just sex, but true love, she felt it in her heart. Knew ig in her mind, and her body wanted to experience all that he had to offer. She already felt that she belonged with him, to him. She felt they were one. So she leaned in and kissed him long and hard trying to convey to him that she wanted what he wanted. This was not what he wanted, he needed her to say the words. So when she pulled back he just stood there, and looked at her waiting. She was confused as to why they had not resumed their walk into the bedroom. He told her to tell him what she felt in her heart. Now, she had long been guarded about her feelings and even though they were friends and she had shared a lot with him she still kept a lot of things locked away. But for the sake of this relationship, she felt she had to make an attempt to say what she was feeling. She started by telling him how scared she was. She knew she had a wonderful friend in him and she did not want to jeopardize that in any way. She told him that she was already in a jacked up relationship and did not want to be doing anything to be considered on the rebound from the situation. She told him that she felt he understood her and would not hurt her but she was still cautious and sometimes it may feel like she was closed away but that she had always tried to keep herself safe and the only way to do that was to sometimes become detached. She was trying to explain all her little moods and in doing so she became so emotional that she could not hold back the tears. He was starting to understand why she had so many mood swings but he knew he loved her enough to hang in there and weather all her insecurities until she finally realized that his love for her was stronger than just merely sex. He wanted her as his soulmate. He needed her just as much as she needed him. He wiped the first of her tears away with thumbs but they began to flow faster. So he leaned down and kissed her eyes. He kissed the corner of her lips. Then, he raised up and as she opened her eyes, he stared at her deeply and leaned back down to claim what he rightfully thought it was, her! He kissed her forehead, her temple, her eyes, her cheeks, and her nose. Now all this was driving her crazy and they were still standing outside the bedroom. He continued with his light kisses, her lips, but he didn't stay there long cause he moved to kissing her neck. He kissed the spot on her neck where her pulse was and at this spot, he added a little more pressure. She moaned and felt like she would pass out. He reached down to scoop her into his arms, carrying her through the bedroom door and gently laid her on the floor. Hse looked at him and asked why she was on the floor and not the bed. He said, "In due time, cause we bout to christen every spot in this room. Can you handle that or do you just want to go to the bed?" Now she was curious and wanted to know exactly what he had in mind, so she said, "I'll follow your lead." He liked the sound of that and continued to kiss her body. He liked the sounds she made when he kissed the pulse spot so he kissed it again. He felt her squirm beneath him and that was almost as much as he could bear, but he really wanted to see if her breast were a mouth full. He had once heard that a mouthful was wonderful and anything beyond that was a waste. He teased the tip of her nipple with his tongue, which caused her to arch her back. He put almost the whole breast in his mouth and began to caress it completely with his tongue. She moaned, squirmed, and arched. Now he really had to enter her because he was throbbing so hard he thought he would explode if she didn't. So he placed his dick at the tip at the tip of her opening in hopes that he would tease her just a little, but just as he placed it at the tip she arched higher and wrapped her legs around him which caused him to fully be engulfed within the warmth of her walls. Now he had to take a deep breath in order to not climax on contact. He wanted to give her pleasure beyond measure.

This was just the beginning cause they went from the floor to the chase at the foot of the bed and then to the bed. This type of lovemaking helped one to sleep and a deep sleep is where she went. It had been so long since she had a good sleep. She slept for moments in time. She would sleep for 30 minutes and think it had been hours. She didn't realize how much she needed this sleep until she awoke 4 hours later refreshed and something like a glow. She felt good from the inside out, she could not explain the feeling but she wanted to talk so she rolled over to wake him but he was not there. She panicked wondering if she had dreamed everything but her body told her no. Then she wondered if maybe she read too much into what had happend all he got out of it was a good fuck and she was on the love making trip. She remembered the conversation outside the bedroom but it was not like she had heard these words before. She had begun to realize that some people said what they needed to say in order to get what they wanted. She was getting distressed but she knew she had to pull herself together and be strong no matter what happened. While she was lying there trying to get her thoughts together and the door opened and he walked in wearing nothing but carrying a tray full of food and fruit. He smiled at her and she breathed a sigh of relief. Now he heard the sigh and put the tray down and asked what was wrong. She just looked at him and he gently took her in his arms to explain that he was not going anywhere unless she told him and really meant it then he would have no choice. He knew what she had endured with Lewis, and did not want her to think he would be a repeat of that in her life. So he looked deep into her eyes and told her that he loved her and that he had loved her for a very long time almost since the moment he met her. He told her that when he first saw her, he had questions about her age and really wanted to get with her, but he had to weigh his options and wait to see if she was available. He told her that once he realized she was in a relationship with someone else, then he had to find out how serious it was, and having found out who she was dating, he knew all he had to do was wait. Patience is a virtue. He knew it would just be a matter of time before things with Lewis came to an end. Now that things had finally come around, he did not plan on losing her to anything like her not trusting or believing him. So, he just sat there and held her. He wanted to kiss her so bad, but he knew that would lead to other things and he did not want her to think that was all that he wanted from her, so he had to show some restraint. He wanted her to know that he wanted an emotional relationship with her more than a sexual relationship. Now he wanted her sexually, but that was not what he wanted to base their relationship on, he wanted her totally. Remember, mind, body and soul. She pulled back to look him in the eyes and at that very moment, her stomach growled. They both laughed. He reached back and got the tray. Now the food was a little cold, so they decided that they would go in the kitchen to warm it and eat at the table. He had prepared eggs, sausage, bacon, and cheese toast. He has strawberries, honeydew, purple grapes, and of course watermelon which was both their favorite fruit. She put on his shirt and as she ate, the shirt opened a little in the front exposing a portion of her breast. He was having a difficult time watching her lips as she chewed and her breast as she breathed. It was driving him crazy. As she was watching him, his eyes darkened with desire. She could not believe she wanted him so badly. She dared not tell him because she did not want him to think that was all she had on her mind. If only she knew that was exactly what he wanted also. He couldn't take it much longer, so he just asked if she was full and ready to go back to bed. She smiled and said she was and he rose and took her hand and led her back to the bedroom. Despite the fact that he wanted her, and he knew she wanted him, he was determined to just lay in bed and hold her. He knew she needed the comfort more than she needed sex. They laid down, and he wrapped his arms around her and told her to rest. She was waiting for him to put the fire out that he started in her mid section and has slowly eased its way down to her inner thighs. He informed her that she just needed to rest, so she lay there and just thought to herself that she felt really happy. That was the last thought she had before she fell fast asleep. She awoke 3 hours later, rolled over and stretched. She purred like a cat because she felt so relaxed. As she rolled, she felt the presence of Frank, however he was still asleep because what she did not know was that he laid there and watched her while she slept thinking how blessed he was to finally have her in his life as a lover and hopefully soon as his wife. This thought caught him totally by surprise because he had never thought himself the marrying kind. In fact, he had long since told himself that he would never let one woman tie him down. Now here he was wanting Tracey as his wife. She raised up on one elbow and watched him as he slept, looking so peaceful. She thanked God for the blessing of putting Frank in her life and letting her finally experience good loving. She wondered how far they could take the relationship if it would ever get to marriage. She knew she wanted to be married and she could imagine her being Frank's wife. She wanted children but she didn't know how many. She wondered if she would ever have this conversation with Frank, but until then, she was content with just watching him sleep. At least she thought he was asleep, but she sighed loudly as she watched him and daydreamed about their wedding and he was awaken to watch her as she watched him. As she brought herself back to reality she realized he was looking at her and she smiled. He asked her what the smile was for and she replied that she was just feeling happy. She leaned over and lay in his chest and listened to his heartbeat. She kissed his chest running one hand through the hairs on his chest and the other down the ripples of the muscles on his right arm. She imagined herself being picked up and held in the air by those strong arms, while he made passionate love to her. She imagined him inside her and could not imagine him swelling within her as she let the juices flow. She knew that she needed to feel him deep inside her but did not want it to appear that she had only one thing on her mind, but in all actuality, that was all that was on her mind. She decided that she would take her chance and tell him how she felt. However, she did not have to say one word because as she lifted her head, he pulled her down and kissed her so thoroughly she felt his heat come through her very skin and made her even more wetter. He reached down and touched her box, rubbing it very softly. This caused her to moan out in pure delight. He inserted two fingers and stroked her clit with his thumb. She put her head back down, as the pleasure spread throughout her body. He continued on this path until he felt her body tense and he knew she was close to a climax. He leaned back to look into her eyes as he brushed his other thumb across the nipple of her left breast. She was so consumed with fire that she thought she would burst. She wanted him to enter her but she could not stop the inferno that was building inside her body and she so wanted the volcano inside her to erupt. She closed her eyes, but he asked her to keep them open because he wanted to see every emotion that crossed her face and mirrored in her eyes. She never imagined that a climax could be so hard without the actual act of sexual intercourse, but the climax that she experienced was so hard she thought her heart had stopped. He was so happy that he could bring her such pleasure. He wanted her to rest for a minute but she wanted to return the favor so she reached out and took his penis into her hand applying firm but steady pressure, occasionally running her thumb across the tip of the head. Now, it was her turn to watch him. He was already deep into the feeling because just watching her had done things to him. She did not have much to do but he knew he would not climax outside her body. He knew he had to enter her before too long. He looked at her and told her that he knew she wanted to bring him as much pleasure as he had just given her, but he wanted her to know that the best pleasure he could be given was for her to lay back and bust her legs open and let him inside. She laughed, but flipped over and opened her legs. The moment he entered she felt the fires start anew and had a feeling this would be a very good and hot moment. He moved back and forth, up and down, occasionally rotating his hips to touch every inch of her walls. It was not long before she called out his name, reaching her climax. This triggered his climax. He leaned down and kissed her letting all his feelings flow into that kiss.

They lay there to rest and while resting, they talked about where they wanted this relationship to go. They both knew they wanted to pursue a serious relationship, but they both stopped short of saying marriage. Frank asked Tracey if she wanted to catch a movie. She did because she wanted to spend time with him other than in the bedroom or sexual act. They had to decide what they wanted to see knowing they both liked action movies.

Chapter 11

Tracey is fixing potato salad, one of her favorite dishes, and in walks Frank. Now Tracy thinks that he is coming to help, but instead, he stands behind her and massages her neck. He feels the tension, so he leans in more and as he is leaning, she feels the outline of his penis on her butt. She is slowly losing control, but she wants to finish the potato salad. She turns around to ask him to let her finish, which is her final mistake because their lips touch and the breath that he breathes on her skin is enough to make her forget the food. She is in ready mode, but Frank wants the potato salad, so he tells her to focus and he will take care of everything else after she finishes.

After she finished, she went into the den to watch television with Frank. He muted the sound because he really wanted to talk to her. He asked what she had planned for the weekend and told her if she was free, he wanted to go somewhere together. Frank wanted to go on a much deserved trip, but she was procrastinating as usual. So he asked her again if they could leave for the weekend. He saw the hesitation in her eyes and she opened her mouth to speak, he kissed her, removing the words from her lips. He leaned back and looked at her and said, "Well?". She opened her mouth to answer but again he kissed her. He planned on doing this until he knew her answer would be yes to them leaving. He wanted to spend some time with her without any interruptions and he needed it to be long enough that she would not think about work, her family or anything that would be a distraction. She had been easily distracted lately and he wanted her full attention. He wanted to pamper her, massage her whole body until it glowed and she smiled from the inside. He wanted to run water in a garden tub, light candles, pour wine into a glass for her and bathe her. He wanted to feed her strawberries dipped in cool whip. Maybe he would even get to eat some cool whip off her body, but that was another issue. He had to control himself so he could take care of her. He knew if she kept pushing herself like this, she would eventually get sick and he did not want that to happen so he was determined to get her away for this long weekend since Monday was a holiday. He deepened the kiss before leaning back. He asked her again but this time he told her that if he thought she was going to say no, he would take his actions to another level and she would be sorry for telling him no. Tracey giggled, she thought Frank was over exaggerating things because she didn't feel tired but she would humor him. She opened her mouth to say no, but decided that she might not like what he would do to her. He could love her to the point of pain because he was good and not giving in to all her desires and right now, after that last kiss, sshe wanted to fuck, but she knew he would tease her and leave if she did not corporate. He had a way of getting her to do things that she didn't want to do but were eventually shown to be for her benefit. She knew he was only looking out for her, but she didn't want to leave town. Despite this, she looked deeply into his eyes and told him yes she would go. He leaned in to kiss her and stopped short of just brushing his lips against hers with a slight brush of his tongue before pulling back and standing to leave. Now she was totally beside herself. He told her that she would get everything she wanted on the trip. He knew he had to keep her waiting because if he gave in, she would change her mind and not go. She had done that to him on several occasions. He would not fall for that trick again. If she wanted the dick, she would have to make this trip. To give her more incentive, he took her hand and placed it on his dick so she could see the seam of his jeans, and he felt that he would explode upon much more contact. But he looked deep into her eyes and said "All this is yours!" Then he turned and left. Now what was Tracey going to do with herself. She had finished the last wedding project and did not have another meeting with any other clients until next week. Here it was, Thursday morning, and she had nothing to do. She started making a list of things she wanted to do on this vacation. She wondered if Frank would even let her do some of it since he seemed so intent on her resting. She thought about that for a minute and decided that she would be really good and do as he suggested because maybe she did need some rest. She thought out loud if he would really make her wait until they were on vacation until he gave her the loving for which her body was aching. Since it was just Thursday, and they would not leave until either Friday night or early Saturday morning, she didn't know if she could wait that long. She decided to bake to relieve her mind.

Tracey is working on getting a cake done for Frank. She has decided to bake his favorite, "Chocolate Cake". She hopes it tastes as good as what he remembers since he told her it had been years since he had one. His grandmother made the last one he had before she got sick and died. His mother never perfected the recipe so she never tried to bake the cake. Tracey is daring and has been told she had the knack for cooking and baking, so she is trying her hand at baking something that she knows he would really like. She finishes the mixing and puts it in the oven. The doorbell rings and since she is not expecting company, she wonders who it could be at this time of night. She does her baking at 12:35 am. This gives her time to put the cakes in the oven and lay down for an hour and thirty minutes before having to take the cake out of the oven. She almost wakes at 3:00. She is trying to get some help but she has so much going on in her head that she just can not sleep for any long period of time. She ask who is it upon reaching the door and it was Frank. He kissed her and she told him to take a seat in the living room. Now she wondered if he would question her stopping him in the living room while she went to the kitchen because he always followed her back when he came over. But the cake was a surprise so he had to stop him and she knew soon enough he would smell it and know she was baking it. She fixed them a glass of wine and went into the living room to sit with him. She knew she would fall asleep so she asked him to just hold her and to wake her at 2:15 am. He turned on some music and sipped wine until she fell asleep. When she awoke, he was not there holding her and she jumped to check the cake, fearing it had burned. He was in the kitchen eating a slice of the cake and she stopped short in the doorway to watch him. He felt her presence and turned to smile at her. She looked at him and asked why he had cut the cake. He said he thought the cake was for him so he helped himself to a slice. She told him that the cake was for a charity event and now that he had cut it she would have to bake another one. He felt bad for a slight moment before he saw the smile that touched the corner of her lips. He went to her and kissed her deeply because no one had ever done this for him. He felt special. She wanted to take her in his arms and make passionate love to her for the deep feeling of care he felt because she bothered to bake the one cake that he loved and it even tasted a little like his grandmother's cake. Instead he just held her close and placed kisses all over her face; temples, eyes cheeks, nose, and lips. He made up in his mind that they would leave at daybreak. He pulled back and asked her what she had on the agenda for Friday. She told him she didn't have anything to do until the next week. He then asked her how soon she could pack. She said she could be packed within an hour and wanted to know why he asked that question. He said that he was leaving and would be back in two hours so they could leave on their trip. He had to get away before he lost all resolve and bedded her.

As Frank was driving away his mind was in a whirlwind as to what he wanted to do with Tracey.. First he had to get her to relax. She had been wanting to get a massage for some time now and despite the fact he really did not want another man giving her the massage that she needed to reach all her muscles and help her truly relax. He also knew that any massage he started would quickly turn into intimacy and there would be no more massage. He would just have to take her to the spa to get the massage and give the guy a look that said she belonged to him. He was determined that Tracey would get some rest and relaxation on this trip.

It was the holiday season and Tracy was not really in the seasonal spirit. Frank wanted her to get more into the spirit of things so he had a few things planned. He planned a week of different activities that were designed to help her unwind. She had been so intense lately with all the Christmas parties she was organizing for everyone else. She was just so out of it but duty called. He did not like to see her this way so he had made up his mind that he and only he could turn things around for her. She had coordinated 3 Christmas parties on the Friday before Christmas and one of the clients wanted her to attend the party. She normally wouldn't go to any clients party because she let her staff handle all that stuff but he had given her an extra one thousand dollars to come and opened his account to her from Christian Dior so she could purchase an outfit. He had even encouraged her to bring Frank. She really wanted to party but didn't want her attitude to upset anyone because one moment she could be happy and the next depression would set in. She was reflecting too much on the past year. She had broken up with Lewis because he had betrayed her trust. She caught him in so many lies and he would even lie to cover the lie after he knew that she knew he was lying. She just didn't understand how he could say he loved her and continue to lie to her. She had started to wonder with all his lying was he also cheating. Now before she caught him and Shempia. Now she had proof and could not see how anyone who lied so much could not also be a cheater. Her family was just not there for her. She had so many little issues trying to make ends meet with the onset of the business "La Cazador". However, no matter how she asked them to help her get the business started no one stepped up to the plate so she was on her own. Now things were looking up, they were always hanging around asking for things. She was usually so accommodating however, lately she had been feeling used. She was happy with Frank but she was still cautious. Her time with Lewis had left her unsure of any relationship. She had grown to know that anyone could say they love you but it took something more to actually say they loved and be able to show and stay committed.

He returned later that night fully renewed and ready to go. He knew they needed to rest for a while before hitting the road at daybreak. She wanted to know where they were going but he did not want to tell her. He knew she could possibly try to change her mind and he knew if she knew little she would be so curious that she would want to go just so she could see what all he planned. He was banking on her curiosity to make her act right and go. He had called and she had not eaten so he had stopped by a local restaurant and purchased her favorite chicken and corn on the cob. He knew she needed some green vegetables so he got a salad with spinach leaves and broccoli. When she opened the door, he leaned in to kiss her and told her to go with him to set the table so they could eat. They sat and ate and had a few glasses of wine. He went to run her bath as she was cleaning the kitchen. He lit a few candles and dropped a few rose petals. He undressed and laid on the bed to await her arrival. She walked in and stared at him. She immediately knew tonight would be one of pleasure. She walked over to him and straddled him as he laid there. She moved her hips in a circle and felt him rise beneath her. She smiled knowing it would not be long before he entered her. A much awaited treat. She smiled and leaned down to give him a sensual kiss while looking into his eyes. She wanted him to know her desires. He lifted her up and rose to lead her to the bathroom. He wanted to wash every inch of her body. He undressed her while paying close attention to each nipple until she was writhing with sheer desire. He ran his hands between her legs and felt the moisture and knew he had to hurry or he would not make it to the tub. He lifted her into his arms and carried her to the water. He lowered her slowly and began to lather her.

They arose early and drove to the airport for the flight to Virgin Gorda. He wanted to explore the quiet coves and walk with her on the beach. He needed her to relax and he knew the next two weeks would be a lot for her with all the parties coming up. They checked into the Biras Creek Resort. As she was getting the massage, all she could think about was getting to Frank. She felt the tension ease out of her body and had him to thank for such a wonderful feeling. She had not felt this good in months- no years. The guy was saying something about the man who had brought her in - how he seemed to love her a lot. She asked him how he could possibly know that and he said it was the way he looked at her. She had never thought about that but as she laid there she realized that Frank did pay her special attention. She closed her eyes and thought about all the times he had been there for her. She realized at that very moment that she loved Frank with all her heart and she was very grateful that he had come into her life. The guy was telling her about the Hot Stone Therapy. "It begins with a dry-brushing, followed by the hot stone massage with warm oil of sage." "It is a deep penetrating heat of the stones that releases tension and nervous fatigue, causing you to experience a more balanced flow of energy." She felt so much energy and she knew just what she was going to do with all of it. That's if Frank could handle what she was dreaming about in her mind. She was going to show him just how much she appreciated the fact that he cared enough to schedule her a massage, even though he had adamantly always said he did not want to think of another man's hand on her body so he always attempted to give her a massage. Now the massages Frank gave were special but this man was making her relax and she felt herself drifting into a deep sleep. She knew he would wake her to go to the Hot Stone Therapy.

She was awakened to a kiss on her temple. She jumped up to slap the guy because she just knew he had lost his mind. As she raised her hand back to swing the blow, it was caught in mid-air. It was Frank who was the one giving her the kisses on the temple. He said he had gotten impatient when it was taking so long, so he asked to come back. The guy had another appointment and she was sleeping so well they didn't want to wake her. He said the guy had told him how tense she was and had suggested that she do the Hot Stone Therapy. Frank did not want to wake her but seeing her on the table looking so relaxed and knowing she was naked under that thin sheet had his mind doing things. He just wanted to kiss her lightly but could not stop at one kiss. She wanted to punch him but instead kissed him. She told him to never come in and have her thinking another man was making a pass at her cause she was about to beat that man to a pulp. She was not going to be taken advantage of and she did not want any massage guy thinking she was an easy mark! He was so proud of her cause this showed that she really cared about their relationship. He knew from this point on, he had nothing to worry about. He still didn't want any other man's hands on her body but at least he knew she would try to take them out if they approached her the wrong way. He smiled - the smile of contentment. She came out looking refreshed and she still had the Hot Therapy Stone. He left out so she could continue. She proceeded to the area for the Hot Stones and was told it would take thirty minutes for the process. She lay on the table and they began to put the stones on her body. She felt the weight and the heat and it felt good. She went to sleep again. When they finished, she went out to Frank and told him that she was hungry but she really wanted to have sweet sensual love. He told her that she had to eat and the lovemaking would come soon enough.

They ate at the Bath and Turtle. She ordered the pasta special and he had fish and salad. They both ordered frozen drinks. The food was delicious. Tracey did not realize how hungry she was until her food arrived and she had almost eaten it all. Frank was watching her and she stopped to notice that she was about to make a happy plate. She could not remember the last time she had eaten everything she ordered and she was even contemplating dessert. She had seen the waiter deliver a cheesecake slice to another table and it looked so good. She was really enjoying herself and she had Frank to thank for it all. She could not imagine it getting any better. She felt relaxed and now she was full. After dinner, they went for a walk on the beach. Just holding hands and enjoying each other's company. They walked back to the bungalow. He opened the door and she saw a table set up with strawberries and champagne. Now she normally didn't drink champagne, but tonight was special so she smiled and turned to look at him. He had a look in his eyes that she could not mistake and she knew that better things were coming her way. He reached out to grab her but she ducked and ran into the bathroom closing the door. She had bought just the outfit for this occasion. It was a red teddy with hot pink trim. It came down just below her hips, covering up the thong that was barely there. She wants to surprise him. He knocked on the door but she told him he had to wait. She listened as he walked across the room ad turned on the television. She jumped in the shower quickly. Drying off just as fast and rubbing vanilla scented location over her body. She put on the teddy and walked out the room. His back was to her so she walked slowly and put her arms around his neck from the back. She leaned in and kissed his neck, while running her hands down the front of his chest slowly easing her way down to his abs heading for his most treasured member. She slid her hands into his pants and caressed his penis. It felt so good as it was enlarging. She closed her eyes and imagined it inside her. Him pumping and rotating until she almost could not take it anymore. Then he would pull back and look at her before ramming into her again, holding her tight. She moaned at the thought. He pulled her around to sit on his lap asking her if she enjoyed her day. She was delighted to tell him how much she enjoyed her day but she thought she could show him better. She leaned in and kissed him deeply. Still rubbing her hands over his pants at the spot just above his penis. He grabbed her butt and she nibbled his ear whispering that she needed to shed some of his clothing. He was all too ready to oblige. He stood and removed his shirt. She quickly kissed his left nipple while running her hands down his stomach. She moved over to the right nipple as he unfastened his pants, letting them drop to the floor. She put her arms around his neck and pulled him in for a kiss while her hips were grinding into him, letting him know exactly what she wanted. He was all too ready. He opened up her teddy and pushed her back just a little so he could admire her body. He reached out and flicked his thumb across her right nipple. She let out a sigh. She knew that if he wanted to take her at this very moment, then she was ready- beyond ready. She felt the juices run down her leg. She wanted to - needed to hold his penis in her hand. She put her hands inside his boxers, taking hold and running her thumb across the head of his penis. She felt the pre-cum juices at the tip and leaned back to tell him that she wanted him. He leaned in for a kiss while removing her teddy and stripping her to the thongs. He removed his boxers and laid her on the sofa. He took a nipple in his mouth while rubbing his thumb across the other one. She moaned and arched her back to bring herself closer to his body. He laid on her and she felt every muscle. He moved a littler to enter her as she lay there looking into his eyes. The movements were slow and sensual, deep and penetrating. He quickened the pace as he felt her calls contracting. He wanted to bring her pleasure before he released himself. He was correct as it was only a few more minutes and she screamed out his name. This triggered his own climax.

Chapter 11

Frank and Tracy had been going hard, making love, fucking, laying back, and going out. Enjoying each other's company. It was a given that Frank and Tracey end up, deeply involved, in a relationship. Tracey was finally yielding to an unfulfilled desire and Frank was getting his desire fulfilled. It was going down, and now that it was, they spent intense quality time with each other. "Fuck it Tracey, lets go to the Caribbean Islands!" "When, asked Tracey?" "Now," said Frank. Without another word, they packed very lightly, and left. Once they got to th4e island and got a room at the Sandals Hotel and Resort, they attacked each other. Everything that they missed in the 2 years they were friends, they were trying to make up for lost time, with the sex they were having. They took a nap for a couple of hours. They wanted to be rested up before they stepped out for the evening. Once they got up and showered, Tracey and Frank, went to the coconut junction, because they both could not imagine traveling to the Carribeans and not trying jerk chicken. In fact, they went to a number of spots. They both checked their schedules and postponed anything they had to do back home, and turned their visit to the islands into a vacation. One day, they took a tour on the sea, it was a clear glass bottom boat so she could see all the elements of the sea without having to get into the water. She knew how to swim but not enough that she was willing to go snorkeling. He knew this would make her very happy to be able to see the animals of the sea. As she was a true animal lover. Afterwards, Frank took her to a place called Mad Dog, where they drank pina-coladas, ate club sandwiches, and ice cream. That night, once they made it back to their room, Tracey put on some music and decided that she would dance for Frank. "Here... sit in this chair," said Tracey, with a mischievous grin on her face. Frank smiled, as he did as she was told. Tracey was dancing to Beyonce's "Dance for You". Frank pulled out a small wad of bills and slowly started to throw them at Tracey, as she slowly and sensually unbuttoned her linen shirt. Frank followed suit and pulled his shirt off and threw it on the floor, as Tracey did the same. Off came the bra. Tracey, seductively rubbing her titties, looked at Frank and turned around and pulled up her skirt to show her thongs and perfectly shaped ass and hips. By now, Frank dick was throbbing. "Take it off," said Frank. Tracey obliged by slowly sliding her skirt off and stepping out of it. She backed up to Frank's lap, sat down and slowly rolled that ass on his already thumping dick, giving him a lap dance. Frank's hand instantly went to Tracey's hio, slowly caressing her hips, as she reached back and rubbed his face and head. This made him kick his shoes off. "Hold up baby," said Frank, as he lifted Tracey off him to shed his pants. He left his boxers on, in the mind of roleplay, to make it more of a reflection of a perfect tease, leading up to some hot sex. She sat back down, straddling Frank, although she couldn't actually dance comfortably on Frank's hard ten inch dick long without wanting all of it up her immediately, and that's what happened. Frank had let his dick out of the hole in his boxers, right when Tracey was turning around to dance on him reverse cowgirl style, "Oh my," said Tracey as she sat down trying to dance. By then, Frank had slid Tracey's thong to the side, stood up, bending her over, and entered her hard, while pounding her pussy like it was going to be the last time he got it. "Hold up baby," said Frank, as he pulled out his dripping wet dick to kick off his boxers and snatch her thongs off, ripping them to be exact. As if he was mad for being teased and hungrily thrust his dick into her, causing Tracey to scream and moan with desire and surprise. Bending Tracey over and fucking her standing up, facing away from the bed, was making the atmosphere change from one levelto the next. Frank noticed the dresser with the mirror on it and saw their reflection, looked at him, and drove him to move toward the dresser. Tracey planted both of her hands on the dresser, arching her back, ready for Frank to put his dick in her, they locked eyes in the mirror, as Frank entered her. "Siss shit!" said Tracey. As Frank slowly grinded up in her, she was rotating her hips to meet his movements. "Damn!" moaned Frank. Because their action was in front of this mirror, it had Frank about to cum already!! He pulled out everything except the head of his dick, trying to prolong his climax. Tracey wasn't having it. She reached back grabbing Frank's dick, as she bagged up on him, that's when Frank grabbed her by her hip and rammed his dick up in her and went pounding and looking in the mirror at Tracey and himself. "Smack, splat, smack, splat, smack" was the sounds that their sweaty body's made as Frank collided with Tracey's round ass. She had on her heel, so that made Frank bust a monster nut! As Frank was cumming, he pulled Tracey's hair, causing her to cum simultaneously. "Ummph, aaaaah" is all the sounds were made in the room, besides the radio. They exchanged some hell of a fuck face in the mirror. Still upin Tracey, he hugged her and made his way to the bed. Guiding Her from the back, not wanting to let go. They collapsed on the bed and slept just like they were.

The next day, they slept late, skipping breakfast and lunch. "F rank...Frank!" said Tracey, shaking Frank, trying to wake him up. "Yeah...Wassup?" groggily said Frank. "Um hungry, and we slept all day," said Tracey! "It's 2:30", said Tracey, as she looked at her watch. Instinctively, Frank looked at his watch. "You right... we need to get up and get something to eat," he said. They kissed as they rose up out the bed, which led to them almost going too far. "Hold up Tracey," said Frank, in between kisses. Tracey stopped kissing him, but her hand stayed on his morning hardness, slowly stroking it, while his hands stayed squeezing her ass. "What?", said Tracy, as she caught her breath. "You're right Frank... Lets get ourselves together." Then she let go of Frank and he let her go as well. They got up and showered together, once they got through and dressed, they agreed upon going to the club house steak and seafood grille. The place speaks for itself. They were about to pig out and wanted the best steak and shrimp they could find. They stayed on the island another two days, and on their last night, they hit Andy's Chateau De Pirate, because Tracey wanted crab claws.

Back in the States

A couple of months had passed and Frank and Tracey were officially a couple. They had started being out together in public more now than ever. They had stopped being evasive about her relationship with Frank among her friends. The only thing they said was "We knew it!" and "It's about time". Everything was going well with them. The only thing that didn't sit well with Tracey was one of Frank's work partners, which was a female sports agent by the name of Angela. And What put the icing on the cake with Angela, was that she fits the exact description of Wendy Raquel Robinson's character Tosha Mack, the female sports agent on the B.E.T sitcom, "The Game". Angela looked like Tosha Mack, shaped like her, and even had that down to Earth but sexy and sassiness about herself. When Frank was going through his training as a sport agent advisor, working with agent's from the school, he got jis certification from Sports Management Worldwide. A lot of times he had to travel with these agents...alone. Angela had been showing Him the ropes when she met with general managers of N.F.L teams, as well as GM's of basketball teams and clients. In Frank's year of working with Sports Management Worldwide, he had learned a lot from Angela about the business. He also learned that Angela was feeling him when they would travel, they would never share a room, and it never was a problem until She would notice a woman had stayed in Frank's room that night and she would show a little jealousy. It was no different with Tracey. Frank had started his own agency, but would still consult with Angela on certain things in the business, and at times, she would pop up on Frank at his office or anywhere. One particular night, she called Frank, as if it was urgent business, while Him and Tracey were at a sports bar. When Angela arrived, and Frank introduced her to Tracey, she kind of put on a fake smile and was not being herself. "Have you ever had her?" asked Tracey, once Angela had left. "What?" said a surprised Frank. " You heard me!' Have you ever fucked Angela?' "Now?", laughed Frank. "What makes you say that?" "The way she looked at me and put on a fake smile. The whole thing was fake with her! Either y'all have fucked, or she wants you. I'm a woman, I can tell." "Ookay," laughed Frank. "Well let me say this... Angela and I have never done anything." "Ookay.. I'm just letting you know what's on her mind, not what's on your." Now it's almost Christmas, Angela sent him an invitation to a Christmas party and he was allowed to bring a guest. They were at Frank's crib when he got it, and Tracey read it also. "Yes, I'm going and I'm going to be your guest!", said Tracey with an attitude. Frank laughed, "I ain't tripping, who else am I going to take?" "Well... I'M going shopping for you and me, just for that party!" And that's exactly what Tracey did. The very next day Tracey had sent some pics to his phone of 2 dresses and shoes. "Which dress? It's going to be red. Just need you to tell me the style. This is the dress I'm wearing to the Christmas party." "Damn!", laughed Frank. "She's on the move." Just as he said that, another media message from Tracey came through to his phone. "These are the shoes," read the text along with the pic. They were some red Louis V's with some small rhinestones. Tracey was in full competition mode against Angela. For what, Frank didn't know, because he didn't have any intentions on getting with Angela. " Oh well," said Frank to himself. "Seh don't have anything to worry about." Just as soon as he said it, there was an email from Angela. She had something to tell Frank. "I don't want you going anywhere with that slut anymore, better yet, I'm making sure I am able to go as well." "Okay baby... I promise, I never hurt going to hurt you. We made it this far now," said Frank, as he kissed Tracey deeply and gently placed his middle finger in Her pussy. She turned around and straddled him, grabbing his dick, and sitting on it, and rode Frank like a maniac.

The Christmas Party had come around, and Tracey didn't really want to go now that she knows Angela was trying to steal her man. The Competition in her wanted to show up and show out. She wanted to show Angela who had Frank. Frank and Tracey showed up at the 10:30 pm, which the party had started an hour ago, so the crowd was heavy. "Fuck," Frank mumbled uder his breath. "What?" asked Tracey. "Now I was tripping on this crowd," said Frank. Actually, Frank was tripping on the short ass skirt that Angela had on. It was red, with some white and green stripes, Christmas colors. It was off the shoulders, tight around every curve and very short with splits on it, with some red six inch pumps on. How ironic Angela was at the door playing hostess, while some of her friends were checking the invitation list at the door. "Fraaank," seductively said Angela, as him and Tracey hit the door. "How are you?" Angela said as she hugged Frank. "I'm doing ok..How about you?" By this time Tracey was fuming. "I'm fiiine!!!" said Angela, being sarcastic. "Umm.. Yes you are right," said Tracey barely shaking Angela's extended hand. "Well, don't y'all look red carpet ready," laughed Angela. Complementing Frank and Tracey on their outfits. "Thank you Angela," said Frank as he grabbed Tracey by the hand, and led her through the crowd. "I'll catch up with you Frank," said Angela, openly flirting. This caused Tracy to almost stop in her tracks and look back at Angela. Which she did look back, and Angela was meeting her graze with a smile. With that, Tracy rolled her eyes, "I don't want to be here long." "Okay baby, we won't," said Frank, as he leaned in and kissed Tracy on the lips.

Meanwhile, Tracy's mother was going through it. She was in a crack house passed out on the floor, still clutching a hot, smoking, straight shooter. To those who don't know, a straight shooter is a broken antennae or something similar, with brillio down in it. It is used to smoke crack on it. The couple of smokers, who was at the table with Elaine, had abandoned her to overdose by herself. She was discovered by a young local dope boy, who stopped by the crack house occasionally to see if anybody was looking for some crack to buy. "Shit," said the crack dealer, when he discovered Elaine laying on the floor. "I hope she ain't dead"

The crack dealer looked at her to see if she was still breathing, he wasn't sure, so he dialed 911, and reported the situation. He gave the dispatcher the address and went out the wide open back door.

"Frank, we've been here an hour, and I'm really not feeling this party." "Can we go now?" asked Tracy. "Yeah baby. I'm feeling that. Well let me go to the bathroom and I'll be ready," said Frank. He got up and made his way to the bathroom. While he was leaving the table, Angela saw that as a cue, leaving her girlfriends, heading in the same directions as Frank. The whole time Frank and Tracy was at the table, Angela passed by a couple of times, at a safe distance. She was watching Frank, and at the same time, she was making sure that she was able to be noticed. She stayed flexing in that short skirt, so that He could see her. She had her back to them, as she chatted it up with her girlfriends, but she had one of them in the circle watching them. So when Frank got up, she was on him, like a hawk on his prey. What Angela didn't know was that Tracy had already recognized her lil moves. So she was on her, but she was going to give her a lil time to see if her woman intuition was on point. Frank went into a stall to take a leak, by the time He had shook his dick, Angela was in the cramped stall with him, like the white woman on the "Obsessed". The white woman, who was stalking Idris Elbai. "What the fuck!" said a startled Frank. Angela had reached around him and gripped his already semi-hard dick. "I know you want me Frank," said Angela, as she slowly stroked his dick. "Hold up Angela," said Frank, but he wasn't resisting much. Truth is, He wanted to fuck Angela baddr than she actually knew. A hidden Unfulfilled Desire. Hidden in his subconscious. He wanted to fuck her, from the first time he saw her, but he didn't want to cross things up by mixing business with pleasure. Plus, now that he was with Tracy, he was trying to be faithful and now Angela is turning up. Angela kissed Frank and still had his dick in a vise like grip, jacking it. Stopping Frank's protest, she quickly dropped to her knees and put all ten inches of Frank's dick in her mouth. "Ooo Angela," moaned Frand, and gripping her by her hair, slowly fucking her mouth. Angela rose up, pulling her panties off at the same time. She turned around and raised her already short skirt up, and Frank gave her what she wanted... His hard dick. He entered her roughly, and slammed all he had in her. "Aaaooo!", moaned Angela. Frank gripped her by her hips as she grinded back, and he started pounding her, pounding her like he was mad at her. He could tell she was about to cum, by the moans, body language, and the way she reached down and gripped the top of the toilet and started throwing it back hard. Like Pusha T's song "Throw that ass in a circle". Frank fket the moaning coming from deep within, like it was uncontrollable on his part plus the mounting tension in his dick. He was so into Angela, that he pulled her hair back, just as he was cumming. That's when he felt the door to the stall hit his back. "Shit!" "What the fuck!" hollered Frank, as Tracy kicked the door. "Oh shit," said Frank, "Tracy! Tracy! Hold up!!" as Tracy stormed out of the bathroom. Angela was smiling. Frank pulled his pants up and went behind Tracy. Tracy had disappeared outside and jumped in the car with Talissa. She had already texted her earlier, and Talissa came on to the party to see what was going on. Talissa took Tracy home and she went in the house, slung her purse, threw her phone on the couch, and just started breaking dishes and glasses. Not paying attention to her blood pressure, she got light headed and fainted.

In the meantime, at the same time, her mother is being rushed to the emergency room... fighting for her life..

To Be Continued..

Book 3 "Police Women and The Convict" (The Wee Song)July 2015

It was one of those hot ass days. We had been grinding all day, cutting grass over at Alabama State University. Now we were headed to the Farmers Market on Fairview Avenue. We weren't tripping. At least that's an hour we can go and kill besides being on campus all day. And then, they don't have much grass to cut over there. I was working on a work squad from prison. Me and 4 other inmates, along with one free world guy who drove the truck. "Damn! Look at that police woman.", said John. "Damn! Shawty bangin!", said Carlos. That's when I looked up to see what all the ruckus was about. "Damn!", I said when I spotted the police lady. "Wee-wee-wee-wee-wee-wee! Got me sanging Lil Wayne and Bobby Valentino!" Everybody started laughing. That was the 1st thing that popped up in my mind. The wee song by Lil Wayne. This police broad has some of the prettiest, brown-creamy skin I had ever seen. She was gorgeous, with some dimples and some serious eyes like a strict teacher. Authoritative, disciplinary eyes like a mother. But it was something behind those eyes. She had the posture like she once had been in the military, but not too stiff. She knew how to be sexy with hers. Then she had the body of a college track runner. Add about 10-15 womanly pounds, meaning she's kind of thick in the right places. Thighs, hips, ass lil over mouth size tits and no waist. You could tell that the few extra pounds came with age. She looked to be about 35, but looked good for her age. You could tell she worked out. Everything was so firm. It was time to flex! She, herself was most definitely in flex mode. She was standing under the pavilion, which was hooked on to the farmers market, in the same building. I couldn't wait to get out of the truck cause I knew we drew attention with the prison whites on. Then I got on this tight ass under-Armour shirt, showing on my physic. I work out regularly, so I'm showing out! Light brown skinned nigga, with a gangster swagger. Fitted hat to the back with some fly ass Dolce and Gabbana shades on. I made sure I was the last one to be seen by her. When I stepped out of the truck, she looked at me and did a double take. I wasn't making it no better because I was flexing. Chest poked out, stomach sucked in. I didn't have no six pack, but I was thinner than the average 40 year old. The dumbbell curls and the back arm workouts got my arms on swole. The kind to make a woman fantasize about being held by those arms. The kind she visualizes being picked up by. The skins she pictures of being put in the buck byb. Police woman was stuck looking at me, so I spoke. "Hey, how you doing?" She nodded and put on one of those "Um being nice smiles." "Good evening," "Damn! She might be jocking.", I said to myself as I grabbed a weed eater off of the truck. I went ahead and worked and tried not to pay her much attention. I finished in the back of the place and when I came back around the front, she was gone. At least that's what I thought until I went on the inside to use the restroom. Once I came out of the restroom, I nearly bumped into her. "Oops! Excuse me! My bad!" "No...you're okay.", said the police woman. And there the both of us were, stuck. "Excuse me, but are you a Lieutenant?", I asked as I pointed at the bars on her shoulders trying to break the ice. "Ah...yes I am.", said the police woman, giving me them pretty teeth and dimples. "Okay...I didn't mean no harm Lt." I paused and leaned in reading her name tag. "Lieutenant Freeman." "No harm taken..um" Now she was kind of leaning in like she wanted to know my name. "Tory.", I said, telling Lieutenant Freeman here my name. "Lieutenant Freeman, you're not going to turn me in for speaking, are you?" Lieutenant Freeman laughed. "No Tory, I'm not. You haven't done anything wrong. What camp are y'all at?" "4-spot.", I answered, pleased that she's showing a lil interest. Niggas in prison day dream about knocking women off, especially if they're put in position to play. A real opportunist, a hustler, his antenna stays up. Waiting for doors to open. "So who do y'all work for?" "Alabama State.", I answered, wondering what's up with this fine ass police woman. So after that, she got into the interviewer mode, and hit me with all kinds of questions. She was acting nonchalant with it though. Kind of like it really doesn't matter, but she's intrigued. Going into the mind of a prisoner was already intriguing to women, but especially if that prisoner was intriguing to that woman on a personal level, and he's a gangster, street with some sense though. And natural charismatic laced with some playalistic flavor. He's the shit! But add some handsomeness, with being in shape. Fine to the women, then you're fire. That's me okay! "Tory! We bout to go!", hollered Carlos. "Well um, Lt. We're about to.." "Andrea..my name is Andrea." "Okay then Andrea..how often you be over here?" I had to ask her. "Wednesday-Friday.", said Andrea. "Okay. maybe I'll see you again, and we can finish our conversation." Throwing the bait out there, seeing if she'll bite. Planting seeds. "Okay Tory. bye!", said Andrea, smiling, cheesing like crazy. "Bye!" The next two weeks, on a Friday we were back over there. But to my disappointment, Andrea wasn't there, until we were leaving. Andrea was pulling up as we were leaving. She made sure she waved though. That following week, I was told that starting that week, I would be dropped off over at the Farmer's Market everyday at 9:00 a.m. to keep things up. Inside and outside. At first I tripped. The supervisors on some shit like, "You've been out here the longest. We know you'll hold it down." Then I thought about it, I'll be by myself, it's laid back and then Andrea! So I played things down, like I really didn't want it, but I accepted it. Besides, it was a chick at E-Z Money, named Sosha, that I'd met about a year and a half prior that I didn't get a chance to taste and fuck. So hopefully I might run into her. Either way I'm playing it how it go by ear. The first time Andrea saw me over there without the rest of the crew, she kind of got excited. Especially when she found out that I was going to be working over there everyday. My first couple of days over there, me and Andrea talked casually, as in passing for 15-20 minutes at a time. The next couple of weeks, morning, started with some type of breakfast and juice and something good for lunch. Sometimes even home cooked meals. With some long conversations learning about each other. I'm doing more listening than anything. At first Andrea wouldn't open up. Then when she let her guards down, I capitalized on everything she was telling me and what I learned about her was that she was terribly lonely. She was a head strong, independent black woman. A police woman, with some rank in a male dominated career. With a military background. An average man had their hands full dealing with her but not me. That's the type of shit that ignites my fire. A challenge. Though it would seem that it would be a challenge.

But it was rather easy to me, because Andrea was choosing. Due to my most undesired position at the time, had her hesitant. But a lil time given, she'll be ready to make a move. Simply because she digs me, and that it would be a forbidden taboo. For a police woman to fall in love with a criminal. A well connected O.G. type of dude. A plus for me, in a way..thena a curse too. A rose comes with thorns. It can go both ways. Especially by me being locked up and a convicted criminal. Oh well, just as predicted, it didn't take long. What sped things up was Sosha. The girl I had met a year and a half prior to date, who works at the E-Z Money, right next door in a mini plaza. I had went to the store, next to her job, quite frequently buying cigarettes and knick knacks, and I ran into her. So quite naturally, we hit it off, instantly. Sosha had started coming to the farmers market, every other day, to talk to me while she buys fruits. Most of the time, Andrea don't be there when Sosha pops up, but this particular morning, Andrea was there. She was outside talking to another officer, when me and Sosha walked outside talking and laughing. I had seen her before she saw us, but I thought little of it, on the strength that nothing was really official with me and Andrea. But Sosha was maybe 27/28 years old, almost a red bone. 5'4', and has a body like a stripper lil waist, and a fat ass. 40-44 ass! With a pretty face. I could tell the way Andrea was looking, she was jealous. Andrea wasn't hard to look at, with a face like Nia Long. Skin tone and all. But the threat was in Sosha's age. Later on that day, I ran into Andrea outside and was kind of acting funny. "Andrea, what's up?" "Ahh, nothing, gotta go on a run.", said Andrea as she walked towards her police cruiser. I didn't say anything, I just watched her fine ass stroll across the parking lot, in a sexy catwalk/track runner fashion. "Damn! Andrea I wanna fuck you!", I mumbled to myself. She must've felt my vibes because she looked back at me and kind of smirked. I still was watching her when she pulled off. She kind of had a frown as she pulled off, but she couldn't help but look at me and roll her eyes. But damn...she was smiling and blushing!

Chapter 2

For the next 2 or 3 days, Andrea was in and out, like she was super busy. So, I didn't sweat her..at least not where she could tell. She acting funny, so I ignored her. This was making her mad. I could tell by the way she looks at me. We still spoke to each other when we're near each other, but I go on bout my business nonchalantly, like I dont give a fuck about us supposingly used to be tight. We were beefing. She was afraid of the way she felt. Couldn't identify with her feelings or she could, but couldn't believe that had almost committed a cardinal offense. Who was she fooling? She had committed, by becoming jealous and childish showing her hand. And the fact that this dude knows how you feel for real now. I later found out, that was fucking with her. To prove myself right, I put myself in position to run into her. In a discreet area, like her office or one of them lil duck off spots. Since she's been beefing with me, I kind of changed up my routine. Normally, I save her office for last, so I can talk to her for a long time. But now, I clean it first, before she even comes to work. Not today though..I'm cleaning it last. When I entered Andrea's office, she was sitting at her desk, playing on the computer. When she looked up at me, it was like she was startled. "Whoa! I didn't mean to scare you!" I said. "No, no. You're okay.", laughed Andrea. "It just...surprised me to see you in here...I mean you started cleaning it before I got here.", said Andrea. "Yeah..I did..I mean I started catching some vibes..you know, that made me give you some space." I said it! Going on and putting it out there. "Ha-ha! Vibes from me?" said Andrea being sarcastic. "Yep! Vibes from you! And since I didn't know what was going on, I just gave you some space." With that, Andrea was smirking, and staring at me over her glasses. Looking me below the waist occasionally, I guess my dick was semi-hard, the reason shawty peeping me like that. I was like that at times, in the presence of a fine woman in an area that's kind of disclosed or secluded. With her being the object of my desire, I'm turned on and up. Andrea took her glasses off, stood up and took two steps and was in my face, "You know why you were feeling those vibes?", asked Andrea. "Why?" "I was feeling some type of way about something." 'Bout what?", I asked, knowing what she was talking about. "I mean, I don't think I should be feeling that I am. But it is what it is. I didn't like when I seen you talking to that female, who works at E-Z Money." Now I'm acting bewildered. "What you mean Andrea? I didn't know it was like that." "Well....you do now.", said Andrea, and next thing you know, we're kissing! Some slow, hot sensual kissing. The kind of kissing that leads to some hot sex, and that's just what it did. After about 15 strong seconds of getting in the rhythm of Andrea's kissing, I encouraged her to get more deeper in the groove by squeezing her ass, as she ran her fingers through my hair. Then all of a sudden, she snatched away. And I'm thinking like "Uh oh!" But to my surprise, she took off the belt with the guns, and handcuffs, etc. she was about to step back into my arms, but I nodded towards the door, for her to lock it. Soon as Andrea locked the door,

I was taking off my shirt. "Damn you fine!", whispered Andrea as she ran her hands down my arms and chest. I pulled her up to me, and started kissing her, and squeezing her firm ass. I started sucking on her neck and unbuttoning her shirt. That shiny ass badge was twinkling in my eyes. That didn't do nothing but make my dick start throbbing hard. The thrill of fucking a fine ass police woman. A lieutenant at that. A bitch with rank! And me? I'm a convicted murderer, slash dope boy! Sliding her bra up to suck her titties, I smiled at her, then she grabbed my dick! She was grinding and rubbing and stroking my dick with aggression. I quickly, but smoothly unhooked my belt and buttons on my pants, to release a pre-cumming dick. She looked down at it, as she stroked it and said, "I don't know Tory..I don't know if I can handle all that!" "You'll be okay.", I responded, as I pulled her tight uniform pants down. She pulled one leg out, and to her surprise, I went down on her! I always wondered what she tasted like. She must have been eating watermelon smoothies cause that's what she's tasting like. "Sissss Tory.", moaned Andream as she wrapped her legs around my head. As I suspected, she had some fat juicy pussy lips. I served her for about 3 minutes strong, making her cum. I raised up and to my surprise, she grabbed me by the hin and kissed me in the mouth. Maybe she wanted to see how she tasted or maybe she's a freak. As long as she my freak and not everybody else's freak. I ran my dick up in her deep and hard, and commenced to pounding. I had her legs wrapped around my neck, her ass on her desk, pounding! Gripping her soft, but firm ass, I'm elated to be on my ti[toes like a dog, going deep into Andrea. As I was about to nut, I looked into Andrea's eyes, and I tongued her down, as we both came. Andrea snatched my cumming dick up out of her, and pulled me towards her mouth. She wanted to catch it. So I obliged by grabbing her by her hair and aiming my dick right to her mouth. "Yum!", moaned Andrea as she sucked at my spitting head. "Shiit!", I moaned, as I slowly grinded and hunched Andrea's pretty face. It seemed she brought more nut up out of me. Like I was cumming again! Andrea just kept on sucking and stroking. Hse was trying to keep my dick hard or she was trying to drain me! Whatever her mission was, I was straight with it. My tool was getting back right instantly. I let her perform on my dick like she was making a movie. After a lil fire head from Andreaa, I bent her over. Palms flat on the desk. I entered Andrea hunrily. "Oooo Tory!", moaned Andrea as she reached back spreading her cheeks to help my entry. I grabbed her by her hips for leverage, and went to work. Andrea's pussy was so good, I almost started singing like R. Kelly on the "Sex Genius" song. "La-la-la-la-la-la-la-la-la-la!" But no! This wasn't an R. Kelly moment, this was the Lil Wayne, Bobby Valentino moment! "Wee-wee-wee-wee-wee-wee-wee!"

Chapter 3 2 years later, November 2017

Riding around the Boulevard in my brand new Cadillac YTS. Fresh to death, feeling myself! I done been free for four months now, chillin'! My relationship with Andrea was cool. It was shonuff some fucking going on between us! She wanted me to move in with her, but I declined. When I was locked up, Andrea rode with me until I got out. We fucked, practically every day we could. Even after I was moved from over there with her, over some player hater shit! But I still can't move in with her just yet. I have to get myself together. Some me time! I just moved to Atlanta and Andrea didn't like that one bit. "So...when did you decide that you were going to move to Atlanta?!", asked Andrea. "I know that you used to talk about it when you was locked up, but I thought that had changed?" I told you, I had to get out of Alabama Andrea! Besides, it's more opportunity for a black man up there. Alabama is a pure prison state. Especially for a black man!" "Okay..I understand that, but what about me? That's what that "me" time thing was all about huh?" Andrea was highly frustrated now. "Well...sort of.", I said. "Sort of?! Tory, it's either it was or wasn't!" "What I meant by sort of..", I went into explanation mode with Andrea, hoping that she would understand. I done came to town to kick it with her this weekend, and I don't want to get off on the wrong foot with her. Besides...the pussy is superb. To go along with her being an undercover freak..I can't let her slip away! Not this weekend. Hot make up sex was brewing on the strength that she was getting mad with me. "Look here baby. I'm on this Blvd and traffic is off the chain. Let me get back to you." "Nawl! Fuck that! You've been talking to me in traffic!", said Andrea. She was 38 hot now. Steaming! She was hotter than a prostitute, who would fuck on credit also!! I had learned that when she's mad, she's also horny. But she said that I had "that " effect on her. That, I hardly believed. "So am I breaking your concentration Tory?" "Yeah, yeah!", I said, trying to make her a little madder. "Hold it..you're trying to be.." "Look Andrea, I'll hit you back!", I said interrupting Andrea and hung up in her face. Now she's really mad! I hope that she don't have me stopped and shit. I don't think she would go that far. At least that's what I thought. As I was pulling over at the Exxon, I noticed this police car going in the opposite direction, whipping around fast in the turning lane as if they've spotted a suspect or something. "Shit!", I said to myself as I pulled up to the gas pump. I acted as if I wasn't paying attention to the police car. I thought it was Andrea, until the car pulled on up facing me. "Damn!", I mumbled to myself. Not because I was dirty or something, but because of this pretty broad! She looked as if she's Puerto Rican or something. I continued to pump gas into my Lac, as I casually looked up at the pretty butter pecan tan police woman. She appeared to be on a cell phone, which wasn't strange. But she was looking at me! Now I know I haven't done anything, and if she was at me, she would be on her C.B. not on her phone. After I got through pumping the gas I went into the store to pay for the gas and got some cigarettes and gum. While I was at the counter, I noticed the Puerto Rican police woman hadn't pulled off yet. She was still parked in front of my car, as if she's wasting on somebody. When she noticed that I was looking at her, she started laughing. Maybe somebody on the other end of the phone said something to make her laugh. Without hesitation, I stepped from the counter and walked out the door to my car and lo and behold, here comes another police car. "Fuck!!", I said to myself. I don't know what's going on, but I think Andrea is behind this mess. "Just be cool!", is what I'm saying to myself. The police car is pulling up behind my car, as I walk around to the driver side, and it's Andrea!! Now the plot thickens! As I look at Andrea I smile, but she's mugging me down and she hits the flashing lights on me! Now my smile is gone. She turns the lights off, but still sits in the car. I notice she's on her bluetooth, so I assume she's on the phone with the Puerto Rican police woman because when I looked back to her, she's laughing. "What's up?!", I asked Andrea, as I raised my arms up like "Whaat?!" She smiled and got out of the car, and so did the Puerto Rican police. "Scared you or something?", asked Andrea. "Nawl...I'm straight! I'm just wondering what's up with you, causing a scene and thangz!", I said letting Andrea know that I didn't like that shit! "Be easy now!", laughed the police woman. "We were just playing with you! Andrea called me to vent. Told me you were in town, and what kind of car you drove, and it was just my luck, I spotted you at this service station. So I called my girl. You got a problem with that?" "Well,,,nawl..I mean..what you was gone do to me?", I asked, returning a flirt, acting curious. I knew that this chick had a pretty ass face, with a braided ponytail, but now that we're up on each other, I noticed how fine she really is! She has a mouthful of titties, lil waist, super curvy hips with an ass that looks like an upside down valentine! Plump, firm, sitting up and poking out! "You know what I was going to do to you?", asked the police woman. "Yeah...I wanna know!" "I was going to handcuff you, put you in this car and take you somewhere and let my friend have her way with you!" "Oh is that so? Mrs..what's your name?" "Officer Lopez!", said the police woman smiling, putting her hands on her hips. Now I noticed Andrea isn't showing any jealousy with the open flirting. Now I'm wondering what's really going on. "Hold up!", I said as I looked at Andrea and Officer Lopez. "Is this some type of unorthodox introduction?" They both laughed. "Tory, this is my close friend Maria. Maria, this is my boyfriend Tory...the one I used to tell you about." "Oh..okay!", said Maria, as we shook hands. I noticed she was looking me up and down like I was fine or something. I looked at Andrea, and she had a smirk on her face. "Tory, where you headed? To see your father?", asked Andrea. "Yeah." "Well call me when I get off. Which will be in an hour.", said Andrea looking at her watch. "Okay." I said as I walked back to the driver's side of my Lac. I couldn't help but watch this butter pecan, bomb, seductive lady, making me drool. She caught me looking at her, and she smiled. I smiled back, letting her know we're on the same accord. She backed her cruiser up a little and pulled on off. The whole time, she's looking at me. Now my dick is hard and thumping, all because of Andrea's friend. Damn, I'm in dawg mode!

After sitting with my pops smoking and talking for about an hour, I fucked around and nodded off for four more hours! I guess that 2 hour ride from Atlanta kind of made me drowsy. To go along with this fire ass honey bud, A Kirt rapper weed. I wasn't even hearing my phone. It was on vibrate, and my pops had done eased away with his girlfriend. "Damn! It's 7 o'clock!", I said when I woke up and looked at my watch I checked my phone, and Andrea had been blowing me up. "Damn!

Let me call my baby. She's going to be tripping." "Hello.", said Andrea. "Hey baby! My bad I had done nodded out." "Booy! I've been calling and texting you! You need to leave that stuff alone!" Andrea knowed that I smoked weed. "I already was kind of tired." "Yeah right!", interrupted Andrea. "Anyway, what's up baby?", I said changing the topic and the atmosphere. "Nothing...me and Maria are just sitting back, drinking a couple of margaritas." "Sounds cool! Can I come join y'all?" "Yeah..come on." That's all I had to hear and I was on my way over to Andrea's. And to top it off, I kept thinking about Maria. What is she doing over Anrea's house? "Well, they are friends.", I tell myself. And that's not unusual, but, we have never hooked up and her friends was there. Due to my past circumstances, I don't think we are supposed to even be involved. So we've always been secret lovers, which was cool. Andrea was into her feelings about me not moving in with her, but instead I moved to the "A". she was actually willing to put her career on the line by fucking with an ex-con. Dick almighty! And I'm her fantasy man. The thug nigga in her life, that she'd always wanted in high school. An unfulfilled desire, that's always been in the shadows, waiting for one day to be fulfilled. I was about to get a treat tonight. One of my fantasies was coming alive also. I didn't know that Andrea was lesbian and Maria was her girl. Maria and Andrea had always been secret lovers off and on. They had met in the military. That's when they first got involved. Both of them love men, so it was hard for either one to be the dominant one. The one to play the man all the time. Neither of them just had bitch qualities, so they both were heavily involved with men. Maria was a recent divorce and Andrea had just broken up with her live-in boyfriend right before I got out. When I got to Andrea's front door, I heard a lil music. Sounds like that Sade! "Hey!", said Andrea. After a slight pause. "Hey.", I answered. "Oh..my bad! Come in!", said Andrea. She was giving me this "Damn nigga you looking good!" look to the point of forgetting to let or ask me to come in. no lie, Andrea was looking good with a short, almost tight green skirt on. Loose enough to let her ass jiggle. When I walked in the den, Maria was sitting on her legs, which was smooth and creamy looking. She had on a black short dress, but hers was gripping every curve she had. I noticed that as soon as she got up to shake my hand. "Hey Tory!" "Hey Officer Lopez. How are you?" "I'm fine. And oh, it's Maria." "Okay...Maria.", I laughed as I took my seat on the couch. Andrea sat on one side of me and Maria sat on the other side. We sat there and small talked for a couple of seconds, then Andrea got up to fix me a pineapple margarita. While Andrea was gone, me and Maria sat there and chopped it up. I found out she was from New York. Brooklyn to be exact. 29 years old. No kids and wanted to eat me alive. It was highly recognizable because she kept giving me the googly eyes and licking her lips and twirling her fingers in her hair. She stood up and flexed on me. "I see the way you're looking at me. You like what you see?" And instantly my dick jumped hard, like times in "29" "Damn! You gone try me like that? You don't have any respect for yo potna!" Maria laughed and sat back down. "If only you knew!", said Maria. I was highly curious. Wondering, is this a set up staged by Andrea or what. No lie..when she flexed on me, I wanted to tell her "Yes I like it, in fact come here!" She had me in instant lust-fantasy mode. Picturing me fucking her from the back. But I killed it. Had to stay focused. These are two police women. So I had to stay up on my P's and Q's cause I'm still a street nigga! A hustler! Instead of just thinking with my dick, I supposed to be trying to turn them into some crooked officers. The game rules! Andrea walked in with the drinks. "I see y'all have gotten acquainted.", said Andrea, "Yeah girl..we have a little...he's acting all nonchalant!", said Maria with a mock surprised look. I casually grabbed my throbbing tool, licked my lips, and gave her a vibe sharing stare in her eyes and quietly repeated.."Nonchalant?" Letting her know that I'm with it. "Yeah, nonchalant.", said Maria. "Not Tory!", said Andrea, as she sat down and kissed me in the mouth, and ran her hands up my inside thigh and grabbed and massaged my dick. She looked at Maria and laughed. Maria got up and got all of the margarita's. We sat there and drunk and talked while Andrea regularly kissed and fondled me through my jeans. I recognized that, that didn't make Maria uncomfortable. Andrea was kind of surprising me. She seems as if she's about to let the freak come out of her, in front of her partner...she did! She grabbed the remote and turned the T.V. to some porn. One dude, and two women. One was Puerto Rican, and the other was black, and the dude was black. And to top it off...the women were in police uniform.

Chapter 4

Now, if my mind isn't tricking me, there is a subliminal message in this whole setting. Maria, Andrea's friend has been flirting hard with me from the intro. Now, we're at Andrea's crib, drinking and watching a fuck flick. A porno-flick, with two police women. One black, and the other Puerto Rican! This wasn't an accident, this was by design, a set up! Okay, if I'm wrong, what I'm about to do now, is going to let me know I'm wrong! I sat there and watched the flick. Letting the movie soak into mind. The alcohol had done loosened me up, and I was in the zone from the good weed I smoked earlier. I already had my arms spread out on top of the couch. I reached out with my right bicep and pulled Andrea in for a kiss. She obliged, with a wet sensuous kiss, tongue kiss. She reached down and gripped my dick. And I immediately unbuckled my belt, unbuttoned my jeans and put my vein filled dick in her hand. I looked at Maria, she was looking at my nine iron, as Andrea stroked it. Maria smiled, and hit her drink, sat it down, and got up. She looked at me and gripped her ass, rubbing it before she walked off. By now, Andrea was turning my head to her by my chin and started kissing me again. Andrea had my dick in her hand, slowly jacking it. I stopped kissing her and aimed her head, by grabbing a handful of her hair to my dick. She looked me in the eyes, before she got on my head, and after a while, I started thinking about what Trey Songs said on that "I love it" remix. "Suck a nigga dick, with a whole lot of spit, let it dripm yeah that's my baby!" I told Andrea that...almost! "Damn baby! Siss shit! Put a lot of spit with it baby!", I moaned when she did it. "Ooo baby!", and her saliva dripped to my balls. To my surprise, Maria walked back in with some lotion. Some motion lotion at that! Sitting the lotion on the coffee table, Maria grabbed her drink, sipped some and sat under my left armpit. I almost head locked her and put that tongue in her mouth. She sat her drink down, and leaned in to really give me some tongue love. She kissed me like she was missing me. She grabbed the motion lotion, strawberry flavor, grabbed Andrea by the hair, interrupting the slow smoking head she was giving me and tongue kissed her. This is about to make me erupt. Seeing my girl, tongue kissing another woman was turning me on majorly! Maria was applying the motion lotion drops at a time all over my shaft, as her and Andrea took turns kissing and blowing it, causing the motion lotion to react. Maria gave Andrea a long, wet, sensual kiss like they've been doing this all the time. Didn't matter. I'm in the moment, hunching Maria in her mouth as I take Andrea's panties off. I take my shirt off and slid out of my jeans and air jordans, swiftly so I can get loose with these freaks. I leaned back into the couch and let these police girls have their way with me. Well not all the way. Andrea got nakes and so did Maria. Andrea straddled my face, while Maria was sucking my dick and licking my balls. I was squeezing Andreas ass as I responded to how Maria is working her tongue, which in turn made me work my tongue! I was licking and sucking Anrea's clit causing her to cum instantly! Maria raised up off my dick for a strong 10 seconds to kiss Andrea, causing her to throw her pussy harder in my face releasing the rest of her sticky down my face. Maria nudged Andrea out of the way, like "Girl you done got yours, let me get mine!" And straddled my dick reverse cowgirl style. She eased down on it, and reached back and put her hands in my chest, and started bouncing on my rod. I knew she wanted this dick when I first met her. Andrea was putting motion lotion on my chest, stomach, arms and sucked and blew it on me, like her life depended on it. I grabbed a grip on Maria's hips and started slamming it up in her! Making that fat ass jiggle. Before I knew it, I was grunting and cumming! At that moment, Andrea was applying motion lotion around my mouth where she had cummed at, and started licking and sucking it off. Boy was I having a treat. A menage trio with two police women.. Fine police women. Freaking them like a porno flick. Maria felt my dick going down, so she got up off of it and started giving me a motion lotion treatment. It didn't take much and I was ready. "Let's hit the bed!", I said. All three of us were moving through the living room in the nude. Once we hit the bedroom, I stood between Andrea and Maria and we fondled each other, I felt guilty. A little because I was showing Maria more attention, but Maria made it right. She started kissing Andrea very passionately. I was kind of getting jealous, watching Andrea's response. It was cool though, living in the moment. She laid Andrea down, kissing her, but regular tooting her ass in the air. I stood behind her, masturbating off of the scene. Maria was sexing my girl down! Sucking her titties, and caressing her stomach. Rubbing in the motion kotion, I was squirting on them both, and masturbating with it. She was playing in Andrea's box, while I stood behind Maria stroking my dick. Andrea looked up at me, as Maria started sucking her clit. I moved over, to where I would be on her side. She looked me in my eyes and grabbed my dick and started sucking it. Soaking all this up at one time. Andrea's reaction to Maria's tongue lashing. The good head she's giving me, and watching Maria do her thang, made me want to bust off! I pulled my dick out of Andrea's mouth and jacked off riht in her face! She let me paint her face! Damn...I couldn't help it! Since I've found out my girl was a freak, I'll have to handle her like one. She didn't seem to mind, so I stuck my dick back in her mouth. We were truly in porno mode. Maria was doing her thang to my girl. She could even suck my dick right. Not without stopping to moan and groan loud as hell. "Uuuuh! Uuuuh...sisss shiit!", moaned Andrea. I got behind Maria and ran up in her. "Aaagh.", moaned Maria. Maria was close built, so the pussy was tight and shallow. In and out side to side, up in her was how I was putting my pound game down. "Yeah baby! This pussy is so good! Damn!", I whispered in her ear. "Ooo papim get this pussy!", moaned Maria. That made me go ape shit. I got up on my toes and started fucking Maria like I was mad at her. I couldn't help but look in Andrea's eyes. I could see the jealousy. She really didn't like how I was enjoying fucking Maria. Well...she did it! I thought of how I would make it up to her. Just as I was about to nut, I snatched out, moved Maria, and dove right into Andrea's wet pussy and came off. That night, I slept inside of Andrea, and Maria slept beside us. I woke up grinding in Andrea and she woke up throwing that pussy back. I was so into Andrea that I didn't notice Maria was laying there with her middle finger in her box, getting off on me and Andrea's sex. After we got through, we all got in the tub and bathed and had another freak session. After that, breakfast and back to bed, but this time we got us some sleep. Sleeping between two fine, police women! "Wee-wee-wee-wee-wee-wee-wee-wee-wee-wee-" And the angels sing!!

Chapter 5

After that menage trois with Andrea and Maria, I got kind of spoiled! I wanted to have Andreaa and Maria at the same time, all the time. We had a few more sexcapades, whenever I came to town. But Andrea wanted me to herself. She was trippin! "Why do you always want me to get Maria when you come see me?!" "I was introduced to you all's relationship! This is new to me!", I said in defense. That;s not answering my question Tory!" "What do you want me to say? Oh you want me to say I enjoy fucking Maria?" "No! I know all that!" "So what's up Andrea?! You introduced me to your lesbian lover!" "She's not my lover! We just.." "Fucking!", I interrupted. Acting like I'm mad. "Well..we're going to slow down doing that with her.", said Andrea. I didn't say anything, I just left it alone. I sat down and started flipping through the television. Andrea sighed and walked off. I know she's regretting the day she let me freaked her and Maria. It came back and bit her on the ass! Because I do enjoy fucking Maria and her at the same time. But I do love fucking Maria! In fact, it had been on my mind to catch her by herself and fuck her! I had her number.

I just never called her. She called me twice looking for Andrea and I locked her number in my phone the second time. "Fuck it!" Keeping it real with myself, I'm going to text her. "Hey wassup!" She text back ASAP. "Nuthin..bored! Wut r u doing? With Andrea?" I lied, "No.. I'm chillin at the Renaissance Hotel..sippin a lil something." About a minute went by before she texted back. "Wow..sounds interesting. By yourself?" "Yes." I know she's interested, likes the hell out of me, and is freaky as hell. "Can I join

?" "You by yourself?" "Yes!" "K." "Give me about 30 min." I immediately went out of the door and got in my car. It didn't take Andrea but a few minutes to realize I was gone. And now she's calling me. "Hello?" "Where are you going? You could've at least let me know you were leaving!" "My bad Andrea. I'm just feeling some type of way. Let me ride and get my mind right. I'll hit you back." I said that, and we both hung up without saying "Bye". "Fuck it!", I said to myself, and flew to the liquor store. I bought some Patron Silver, and some cranberry juice and a 6 pack of Coronas. I went to the Renaissance Hotel and rented a room on the 10th floor. I text Maria the room number. "Room 1030." After about a minute, Maria texts me. "K..on my way." I hit her back, "Bet!" I sat around and smoked a mini cigarillo of loud and drank a Corona and flipped through the TV waiting on Maria. My mind was running 100 miles per hour. I was thinking what if Maria is setting me up? "What if Andrea popped up with her?" "Calm down Tory.", I said to the empty hotel room. Whatever happens, happens. I left the tv on the porn channel. Some black guy fucking a brazilian woman from the back. That shit was getting me horny watching it. And just in time it was a knock at the door. I peeped through the peephole and it was Maria. With her fine ass. "Here goes nothing.", I said as I opened the door, half expecting to see Andrea bust around the corner. "Hey baby, what's up?", I said as I let Maria in. She had on a short tight khaki skirt with a tight white shirt with two buttons on it. She had her hair pulled back in a long braid. "What's up Tory? What you been smoking in here?" "Oh a lil cigar.", I said smiling, "Yeah..what was in the lil cigar?", asked Maria, returning a mock skeptical smile. I was pouring Maria a drink by now. "Here. Lighten up" I gave Maria her drink and was eye to eye. Kind of stuck. "Whuuut?"said Maria, smiling. "Damn you pretty!", I said, then grabbed my drink and sat down. Maria sat down beside me. "So what's up? Where's Andrea?" "She's at the crib.", I answered. "So..why she's not here with you?" "I don't know. Why y'all not together?", I asked. She sat there for a moment, looking at me with a smirk on her face. "Well...you're her man. Y'all are supposed to be together!" I looked at her for a moment, smiling. "I want to be with you, one on one. How about that?", I said it and downed my drink. As I reached to pour another drink, Maria grabbed my arm, lightly and leaned in for a kiss. I tongued her passionately, causing her to put down her drink and moaned. "Why you moaning baby?", I asked between kisses. "I don't know papi...it's good!", said Maria. I kissed her a few more seconds and fixed my drink and fixed her another one. We sat there and took a few hits from our drinks and watched the fuck flick. Maria was sitting all up under me. "So why do you want to be by ourselves?", asked Maria. "I don't know..it's something about you...and Andrea don't want me to be in another menage trois with you. So I figure, maybe we can chill together, by our lonesome." "By our lonesome.", repeated Maria, as she laughed. "Yeah..I know.", said Maria. "You know?", I asked. "Yeah...she kind of mentioned it to me..and also, I can tell how passionately you fuck me.", said Maria, putting emphasis on "Fuck me.". Said it kind of hard, to the point of making me want to get it in her now. To go along with her accent, she had me going. So I tongue kissed her, to kick this shit on off. "Mmm..what's that for?", moaned Maria. I kissed her hard and slow before I answered. "To get you ready for something passionate, and I ain't talking about the drink." Maria started laughing at that and threw her arms around my neck, and started kissing me. Not wasting anymore time, I ran my hand up Maria's thighs, around to her ass and squeezed it. I don't think she has any panties on, or either she has on a thong. I was steady kissing Maria and I ran my right hand from her ass, across her hip, to that pussy, and I was right. She didn't have a lick of panties. "Aah!", moaned Maria, as I caressed her. She was already good and wet. Maria made it her business to reach down and grab my dick. And I made it my business to release it from my jeans. For her to grab it. "Hold up baby.", I said to Maria, as I proceeded to get naked. She swiftly did the same. I got up and turned the lights off and left the TV on and got straight to it. I pushed her legs back and went head first to that box, which was pulsating. She was almost dripping wet. "Mmm-ooo--siss-oh my God! Papi!", moaned Maria. I was eating Maria's twat like dude on the flick, which was on TV at the time. I sucked andlicked that pearl tongue so good, that it didn't take no time for her to cum! "Ooo, oh my God! Tory!!! Torr, ooh, ooh, sis, ooo, Paapii!", screamed Maria as I did my thing. She was leaning up and grabbing my hair, scratching my shoulders trying to pull me up. Acting almost like a woman having a baby, as she let her river flow. "Ooh please baby! Fuck me! Siss, put it in please!!" Obliging to Maria's lust filled moanings, I raised up and rammed my throbbing dick up in Maria. "Aww-oh..siss, yes papi!",screamed Maria, and I only had my head of my dick a third up in her. She was thrusting and grinding and winding her hips trying to get the rest of her juices to flow. Good wet, but tight, close built, shallow pussy. As I slowly raised my ass to hunch and go deeper in Maria, she started caressing my back, to my lower back. We commenced to fucking slow, but hard. As we sped up, I grabbed the mattress for leverage, as Maria wrapped her thighs around my back, expertly. Maria was gripping my dick with her muscles, and throwing the pussy at the same time, causing me to cum hard! I was experiencing some heavy breathing. This woman had me trying to catch my breath. Actually trying to hold back a nut makes the feeling more intense. If you let it go too far. In which I did. I grabbed her by the bend of her knees, pent her thighs to her side, ankles up to her ears and started dropping down in her till I was bustin 'off! "Grr-grr!" I was grunting and growling that nut up out of me. "Shiiit!" I moaned. "Yes papi! This pussy is yours.", whispered Maria, and that made me grind in Maria's box even harder! Matching her motion, in sync with her, I got back right and started back diving in her, up and down, with perfect timing. This fine puerto rican, got some A-1 snapper pussy, and she's motivating me to fuck her all night, and that's what happened.

Chapter 6

Waking up inside of Maria was an instant aphrodisiac. So quite naturally, we fucked. We were all tangled up. But I was stuck in her like a dog get stuck in a female dog. I was laying from the side (kind of). My right leg was over her left leg, my dick was still up in her. Her right leg was across my right side of my stomach. When I woke up looking at Maria's face, I gently started grinding in her. Within seconds, she was slowly grinding back and moaning. I lifted her right leg up, planted my right foot, and started thrusting hard in Maria. Just as I was about to nut, I grabbed the headboard with my left hand so I could bang this pussy good. "Oooo shit!", I said, as I was cumming. After giving Maria a little of my seed in her pussy, I snatched my dick out and moved to Maria's face, and jacked the rest in her mouth. She was catching it like a pro, and sucking me so good, that I slowly but deeply stroked in her mouth, like I was hitting the pussy. "Ooh shit! Girl you gone drain me!" I said as I rolled over. Maria smiled. 'Wel...good morning to you too!" Maria and I got up and showered together and went our separate ways after dressing. We both agreed to do that more often. Hooking up solo. The pussy was bomb, and she seemed like a down ass bitch on the low. The wheels had been turning in my head, about the whole situation. Me, a thug nigga, fucking two police women. How could I get more out of the situation, than me just fucking two fine police women? Could I start some inside info, on what's going on with the local law enforcement? Me being a hustler, I need to know what's up! I have people down here who hustle. I can pull their coat tails if I hear something. I got to start asking questions. Three days had done passed and Andrea had not called me, and I hadn't called her. But I had been talking to Maria faithfully. Matter of fact, Andrea's name wasn't mentioned one time. And we are on the phone now hooking up. "Wassup? What club y'all at?" "Da Terrace. Why don't you come on down..I got someone I want you to meet.", said Maria, trying to talk over the music. "Oh yeah?..A female?" "What do you think?", said Maria, being sarcastic. "Female Tory. A good friend of mine." "Okay give me ten minutes." I had a suite down at The Embassy. So I was right around the corner from the club. The club they were at was kind of upscale. A lot of jazzy bitches be in there, so I got to be on my shit with my dress game. I had on a Versace fit, with some Versace frames, Versace chain, and some fy ass Mauri gators. Not the old kind, the new school. I had been moving dope since I was out, so dressing in high end fashion, here and there wasn't a thing. I think Maria had an idea what I did. Just as well as Andrea, but they weren't for syre. The only way to reveal that is these cops will have to be on some helping me further some conspiracy type shit. Down for the cause. If not, they'll never know. Once I showed up feeling high and mildly tipsy, off some ciroc, it was on. I hit the door swagging, as I casually scanned the crowd. Letting these women know in a non verbal way, that I'm with it. Just like that, old UGK song, "Bitches stare a nigga down when I step to the bar!" That's exactly how it was when I stepped to the bar. On my way there, I almost bumped into this fine ass redbone. "Oops! My bad!", I said. When I looked at her, she almost took my breath away. I thought it was Lisa Raye. she had the eyes, the lips, which is intriguing me, and the shape! Ass and all! "No you're straight.", smiled the Lisa Raye look alike. Her voice even sounded like hers. With a hit of a Latino accent. She had on a tight purple skirt. "Damn!", I said as the woman looked back at me, smiling as she walked off. I went on to the bar and ordered me a double shot of Ciroc, and a Corona. I walked around the club, admiring the sight of all these fine ass women, until I walked up on Maria at her table with the same Lisa Raye look alike. "Heey! Wassup!", said Maria, as she stood up and hugged me. "Heey! Wassup!", I said, as I was hugging Maria, yet looking at the Lisa Raye look alike. And she was looking at me! Maria looked back at her friend, and then me. "Oh Tory, this is my friend Kalisha. She's from Chicago. Kalisha, this is Tory." "Nice to meet you Kalisha.", I said with a smile, as I shook her friends hand. "Nice to meet you Tory! You're the one that almost knocked me down at the bar!" "I apologize!", I said. "No, I'm just kidding!", said Kalisha. I was mesmerized! She had these almond shaped, light brown eyes. Pretty ass smile, and lips! "Well have a seat Tory!", said Maria as she got up and let me sat between the two of them. "I know you've heard this a lot, but you look just like.." "Lisa Raye.", said Kalisha, finishing my sentence for me. We all laughed. "Yeah, I've heard that a lot.", said Kalisha. "So what are y'all drinking?", I asked. "Um,.get us a pink Moscato on the rocks.", said Maria, as she looked at Kalisha for approval. I got the waitress and ordered their drinks. We sat and chit chatted awhile. I found out Kalisha was a detective who had just moved from Atlanta. "Damn! More police!" I was thinking this to myself. Coming from where I'm from, the hood and years of being incarcerated, this shit was awkward. Being around the law was a no no for niggas like me.

Even if we're not violating. Well, at least they're some fine ass women. And I'm having a ball fucking Maria and Andrea. Right now, Andrea was another story. Kind of out of the picture. She's been acting crazy lately, so I've been giving her some space. But in the meantime, I'm trying to see what's up with kalisha. Is she with the freaky shit like Maria? Is she strictly bout the dick or what? Well, time will tell. I hope she's not some type of broad working on a big case. An investigation with an Atlanta Montgomery hook up! Well, they don't know any of my business, at least I don't think they do. "So..Tory, what do you do for a living?", asked Kalisha. And she asked the million dollar question. "I'm a small business owner.", I said, which was the first thing that came to my mind. "Oh...okay! You mind me asking what kind of business?" Maria was cutting her eyes at me, smirking, like she knew I was lying. And the wheels in my head is turning like hell. I'm stuck between impressing this Lisa Raye looking queen, and not say the wrong thing in which would raise some red flags. "I'm into real estate.", I said "Oh really?!", said Kalisha. This caused Maria to look at me with raised eyebrows. "Yea!", I answered and went into some small talk about real estate. I could tell that she had a lil knowledge about real estate, and it was good that I did a lot of reading in prison and gained some knowledge on real estate and other things. If not, Kalisha would've tripped me up, and knew that I was lying. I swiftly got her off the subject, and kept the conversation flowing. "So what kind of detective are you?", I asked. "Narcotics.", answered Kalisha, with a devious smile, to go along with those devious, but pretty eyes. Like she know I was a dope-boy. It didn't matter, because I was lost in those eyes. "Okay...interesting!" I said. "Yeah...it is.", said Kalisha. "What's wrong?", asked Kalisha. "You got this look on your face!" I wanted to tell her how bad I wanted to fuck her. "Noo! I'm cool!", I said. "Come on let's dance!", said Maria, looking at Kalisha, as she rose up out of the booth. Kalisha got up also. Holding and returning my stare. "Well...come on.", said Kalisha as she grabbed my hand. I got on up, even though I don't really dance, but to be close to Kalisha, I'll jig a little bit. Maybe the dancing and alcohol would help her get up on it. Laughing to myself, "With yo dog ass! You trying to fuck yo girls friend with yo dawg ass!" Wait a minute, that's where I got my girl Maria from, my girl Andrea! Which was Andrea's lover and friend. What a life! I'm out on the dance floor grooving, dancing between Maria and Kalisha. They got me in a sandwich. I got my drank in my hand, trying not to waste it on Kalisha. I was facing her, till she turned around and started backing that ass up on me. "These hoes wit it!" First thing hit my mind as she was grinding her fat ass on my hard dick. Maria turned me around, and started grinding her ass on me. We danced, and touched and grinded on each other about 4-5 songs. By now, my dick is throbbing which in turn cause the wheels to start turning in my head. "More drinks?",I asked the girls. "Cool!", said Maria and Kalisha in unison. We went back to our booth, called the waitress and ordered our drinks. I got another ciroc and cranberry and Maria and Talisha ordered the same. We sitting down in our booth and I'm back in between them, flirting with my arms almost around both of them. "Can't wait to taste y'all tonight.", I said to Maria, but loud enough for Kalisha to hear it. "What did he say?", asked Kalisha. Maria was laughing, while I smiled. "No, I missed something! What did he say?" "He can't wait to taste us tonight!", said Maria to Kalisha. Kalisha leaned back and looked at me like, "Nigga what?!" With her eyebrows raised. "Look..I apologize if I offended you!", I said, in a very sincere tone. "Nawl, you cool! It's just that..you don't even know me to be even putting that in your mind..and then just saying it!", said Kalisha, as she's shaking her head in disbelief, but yet smiling. She shrugged her shoulders and said, "Y'all country boys just bold like that!" "Whoa..now that ain't cool Kalisha.", I said as I laughed. "See what you did Maria?!" Putting Maria in it was cooling any ill feelings, but yet warming the pot up for some possibilities of some hot sex tonight. "Whaat!? I didn't have anything to do with what came out of your mouth!", said Maria and we went from there, talking, laughing, and partying for the next couple of hours. Maria had to drive for me! I was semi drunk. Not sloppy, but I was scared to drive. Don't need no D.U.I.'s. We followed Kalisha to Maria's place. She got out of the car in a hurry, like she had to go pee or something. The whole time she's walking to the door, I'm watching her ass! The way she move with it, and the way it bounce, is turning me on like crazy. "What's up with yo partner Kalisha?" Maria looked at me and smiled. "What you mean what's up with her? You want to know if she's a lesbian?" "Yeah! Is she down for a menage trois?" "I don't know." Mari thought she had read my mind. Well...partially she did, but I had more in mind. "I mean, is she cool?" "Yeah she's cool.", said Maria. We went into Maria's house, just as Kalisha was coming out of the bathroom. Just as I thought, she had to piss bad. "Heey! Are y'all too wasted that you can't drink anymore?", said Kalisha as she pranced off to the kitchen. Me and Maria took us a seat in the den. Before I knew it, Maria was grabbing my chin to kiss me. "Ummm-umm. What was that for?", I asked. Maria giggled. "What was that for?", said Maria mocking me, as she stuck her tongue deeper in my mouth. I obliged by returning her kiss, and gripping her ass at the same time. Kalisha walked in right when I was cracking my eyes open. I looked her dead in her eyes, still kissing Maria, wishing it was Kalisha. And Kalisha knows this. I can tell the way she smiled. She had a bottle of New Amsterdam Vodka, and a bottle of cranberry juice. She left out, to go get three glasses with some ice in them. "Y'all come up for some air now! Are y'all drinking with me?", said Kalisha as she poured the drinks. We sat there and drinked and talked till all three of us were drunk. I reached and grabbed Maria and started kissing her. She reached and grabbed my dick, and I started rubbing between her legs. As me and Maria sat there, fondling each other, Kalisha sat there and watched. "Can't y'all go in the bedroom with that?" I looked up at her, and she had this fake look of disgust. I smiled at her and grabbed Maria by the hand and she led me to the bedroom. I hugged her waist from the back, pressing my hard dick on her ass. Kalisha watched us leave the living room with this mischievous, but sexy look in her eyes. When me and Maria hit the bedroom, we were undressing each other quickly. Drunken love in effect. When we got undressed, I was all on Maria. Hungrily kissing her and laying her on the bed. My mind was dead on Kalisha though. Wishing this was her I was laying down. My imagination was running wild. I started picturing this was Kalisha I was sucking on. I guess Maria was thinking that the alcohol had me all over her like I was, but the honest truth was, Kalisha had me stirred all up! As I was entering Maria, I was picturing it was Kalisha. "Ooo Papi!", said Maria as I pent her legs back. Making her knees touch her elbows, I was dropping dick deep into her and tongue kissed her at the same time. This was cousin the stars to fall. "Splat-splat-splat-splat-splat!", was the sound of our semi sweaty bodies as they collided. "Sisss...uggh!" I groaned as I pictured emptying my seed into Kalisha instead of Maria. "Ooo papi! That was great!", moaned Maria as she continued grinding on my dick. "Uh-uuggh." "What the fuck!", I said looking back at Kalisha clearing her throat, leaning in the doorway. "That's all y'all got?!", laughed Kalisha. Then she halfway staggered in the room to the bed. I knew that Kalisha and Maria probably been getting down, so I really don't know how she's feeling about me fucking Maria. So I got up off and between Maria's legs to see what's up with Kalisha. Is she a threat or what? "What's up Kalisha?" "What you want to be up?!", said

Kalisha, being sarcastic. But making my dick hard. I didn't even cover it up. I just laid back, and let my soldier stand at attention, wading at her, like a cobra, ready to strike. She was looking at that mufucka, as she leaned into Maria, kissing her. Oh my God! She's with it! Just as I hoped. I laid back and watched them kiss. Kalisha was digging in Maria's pussy, while Maria pulled Kalisha's skirt up to grip that juicy ass of hers. I'm loving this shit! A convict's dream come true. This the type of shit niggas in prison fantasize about. I was stroking my dick the whole time they got each other hot. Kalisha straddled Maria, after Maria tore her purple thong off. The whole time Kalisha was kissing Maria, she's opening her eyes, looking at me, while I gun them down. That's prison slang when an inmate is masturbating while looking at a female prison guard. Now I'm gunning down two fine ass female police officers. Naked though. I didn't want to waste this nut, so I had to get in the groove with Maria and Kalisha. Specifically Kalisha. I slid over to get close to the two and it seems as if Kalisha was like a magnet to my iron. She smoothly slid off of Maria in the middle of a kiss, and into my chest, kissing me like she misses me. Returning her kiss, and inserting my rod into Kalisha was almost mind blowing. Her pussy was a perfect fit to my dick. Like a hand in a glove. She put her hand in my chest and started grinding on me in a very sensual but aggressive way. All I was doing was picturing this was Lisa Raye. Without my eyes closed. Because she looked so much like her, I could just look in her face, and use my imagination. Getting lost in her eyes was making me lose control. To me, it seems as if she was losing control also. The way she was gripping my chest, heavy breathing, closing her eyes, and rolling her head in ecstasy, made me grip her ass and started stroking hard. She started bouncing on my dick, matching my thrusts caused both of us to cum hard as fuck. I rolled her over, and laid between her legs grinding and kissing Kalisha like she's my girl. I had to get back right, to sho nuff get this pussy some more. It didn't take me long to get back right in the groove of things. Second wind intact. Drunk, but focused. Beast mode. Maria had done passed out. Now Kalisha has all of my attention. "You want me don't you?", asked Kalisha in between kisses. "It seems to me, I got you right now!" I said as I put her legs on my shoulders and commenced to pounding. I fucked Kalisha and passionately made love to her all over Maria's place. The next morning, I smashed Kalisha before leaving. She walked me to the door and gave me her number. "Look..call me later on today..okay?" "Okay..what do you and Maria have planned for today?" "Nothing...I probably won't be with Maria."m said Kalisha with that mischievous smile I'm beginning to love. "Okay..that's what's up!", I said as I walked off.

Chapter 7

Andrea had been acting crazy as fuck lately. I don't know if it's the fact that I haven't been giving her more time lately or what. Especially she knows that I've been back and forth to town more and I stay longer than normal. Instead of just staying the weekend, I might stay the whole week! "You've been coming to Montgomery and staying longer a lot lately. Where you been at? You don't be with me! And I know you have friends around here, but you can't be with them that much!" Now I'm feeling some type of way, because I thought she said about a month ago that she had done linked back up with her ex. And ever since that night, I left her place, to go hook up with Maria, we've only hooked up or talked very little. When we did talk, she acted as if she's irritated, or I'm doing or saying something to irritate her. I don't know what the business is with her, but my patience has ran thin, so fuck it. I'll give her some space, if that's what she wants. I'm a dawg anyway! After that night at Maria's place, I was seeing more of Kalisha. Maria didn't seem to mind. We were still having three-somes, but me and Kalisha were hooking up one on one like me and Maria had started doing. When I started doing the one on one thing with Maria, it wasn't all that personal, it was more of a lust thing and something to do. But with Kalisha, it seemed as if we're drawn to each other by some cosmic force or something! Because it's magical every time we hook up. Even when we just see each other in passing in a restaurant, store, etc. We can't be seen, fraternizing much, because he is a detective and I am a hustler. We still managed to hook up. After weeks and weeks of our secret rendezvous, shit had gotten serious with me and Kalisha. "Tory, I have a question for you.", said Kalisha with a serious look in those Lisa Raye eyes of hers. "I'm all ears. What's up baby?" I said as I stroked her hair. We had just made love, and she was laying on my chest. Rubbing my shoulders and arms. We were having a pillow talk. "I want to know where do you see yourself in the next 5 years?", asked Kalisha, "Damn..where did that come from?", I said, kind of surprisingly. "Me! That's where it came from?", said Kalisha. "I mean...what made you ask me that?" "I don't know..I was just wondering. Now answer the question Tory." "Well...I see myself as a wealthy entrepreneur in 5 years." I saw a spark in her eyes. "A wealthy entrepreneur.", she said slowly."Yea..why did you repeat it like that? It's like you're measuring my words or something. What..are you weighing what I said on a mental scale or something?" "Well..kind of.", said Kalisha. I laid there, looking those pretty eyes for a couple of seconds, trying to guess where she might be going with this. "Where do you see yourself in the next 5 years?" Kalisha looked in my eyes, as she continued to draw circles in my chest. "Well..I'm waiting.", I said, and kissed Kalisha. "Well...I see myself as a wealthy entrepreneur also." I laughed at that. "Why are you laughing? I mean..what's funny about me wanting to be a wealthy entrepreneur? What? Is it because I'm a woman? Oh I get it. Niggas like you feel like since I'm a police detective, I don't make enough money." "Hold it, hold it. I didn't say any of that. and what do you mean niggas like me?" "Tory I know that you're a hustler! Now ask me howI know?" I just smiled at that statement before I responded. "O kay..how do you know?" "I am a narcotics detective for one." "And?" "And..I been did a background check on you. Thoroughly." I laughed a little to hide my sudden nervousness. What is she telling me? "So what's up? I'm under some type of investigation? Secret indictment or what? What does this got to do with where you see yourself in 5 years?" "Whoa! No need for the hostility.", said Kalisha, because now I'm sitting up on my elbows, and I'm not smiling. I'm almost about to get up out of bed with her! "Okay..so what's up?" "I had to see what type of nigga I'm dealing with. In the field I'm in." "The field you're in? Look..you're spooking me now baby! What you mean the field you're in? Kalisha you are the police!" "That's not what I'm saying.", said Kalisha. "Okay, fuck the dumb shit. What you done found out about me? That I done been to prison?", I said, almost heated. "Yes..also that you're in the game. But be cool, let me hip you to something.", said Kalisha. "Well stop beating around the bush Kalisha! What you done heard? Hip me!" "I'm in the game too!", said Kalisha. I'm quiet now. Because not only has she surprised me, but I'm curious as hell. Is this some type of set up or what? I was wondering how she had this big ass house in Arrowhead, and was pushing a brand new vet and new Range Rover sport. "You're in the game? What you mean you're in the game? Enlighten me" "Dope game Tory." By now, I'm sitting all the way up. My back up against the headboard. "Dope game?", I repeated, as I looked at her in a suspicious way. "Nawl...dope game!", said Kalisha as she twisted those lips up being sarcastic. I had to kiss those lips when she did that. "Yes Tory! Dope game! Specifically coke game and a lil heroin." I was astonished. "Damn! You're serious?", I asked. "As a heart attack.", said Kalisha. "I mean..how do you do that? Crooked officer!", I said with a smile. Kalisha punched me in my arm.

"Well..I haven't been doing anything in Montgomery, but I still have something going in Atlanta and South Carolina." That made me look at her with raised eyebrows. "Damn! Who you know?!", I said. "Right now, chill with the questions. I'll fill you in later.", said Kalisha. "But that's why I had to see what type of dude you are. Even though I found out very little from my own lil investigation." "Okay..now I want to know how you found out that I'm allegedly hustlin." "Simple...yo friends or associates, here in the Gump.", said Kalisha. "I only have a few friends or associates here in the Gump. i fuck around with a lot of women though." With that being said, Kalisha frowned at me, and made one of those "Oh yeah" faces. "Well, we ain't gone mix business and pleasure Playa!", said Kalisha, putting emphasis on playa. "What I want to bring you in on, you got to be on point. And what you do with your dick has nothing to do with it. Oh..unless it's in me."m said Kalisha, as she grabbed my tool and stroked it. "Besides, them other hoes ain't got shit on me! So what's up?" Kalisha was sly in seducing me. Because she can see the dollar signs in my eyes and she knew I was feeling her. "You still ain't told me about my friends and associates," "You kind of walked into a stake out, when you visited a guy named Vito." "Damn!" I thought to myself, keeping a poker face. It still can be a set up. "Who is that?", I responded, playing dumb. "Come on Tory, it's on video of you pulling up to Vito's brother's house in that same Cadillac, which is parked in my backyard now! Don't worry y'all was just talking. Standing in the yard, smoking." "Damn!", saying to myself, as I raised up out of the bed naked. "What's wrong with you?", asked Kalisha. I was grabbing my boxers and putting them on. "Is he in any danger?" "Not really. His name has just been ringing on the northside, so the department was doing a lil light check on him. He's not under no heavy investigation, and neither are you! Baby I'm on it! You don't have to worry about shit in that area. I got you! I fuck with you Tory! And if ever I know your name or any of your partners name is in something, I'll put you on game. I won't let anything happen to you. Trust me. Right here..okay?" Now I'm standing here holding my polo jeans about to put them on. "So what's up Kalisha, what are you trying to do?" My curiosity took over. "I'm trying to put you on, if you'll let me." I gave her an "Oh yeah", then "Yeah right" look. "Okay! I'm tired of you underestimating me/ what are you working with?", said Kalisha. I can tell she was irritated now, so hse might be serious. I still feel funny about telling her what and how much I was copping. "I've been fucking with weed mostly. Mid and loud and a lil blow." "Weed mostly, mid and loud and a lil blow.", repeated Kalisha, as she was in deep thought. "Look baby..I can get all of that for the low. You're just being so evasive. I understand what's going on with you though. Trust issues. I understand, but let me show you something.", said Kalisha as she got up and put her robe on. "Follow me." Kalisha took off down the hall and went into one of the guests rooms. Went to the walk in closet and swiftly took a left and a quick right under some coats. "Damn girl. Where are you?", I said, slightly startled because I know it's a wall there. Then before I knew it, she emerged from behind me. "What the fuck?", I said. "Damn..how did you do that?" Kalisha laughed. "Secret passages.", she said as she turned on a light in the closet. "Here, take a look." Kalisha was handing me a Louis V carry on bag. I looked at her kind of hesitantly before I opened it, and damn, there's two bricks of cocaine. I pulled them out of the bag and looked at them. By the looks of them, it was some fish scale. I was smiling, looking at the work, wth dollars flashing like a machine at the casino in my eyes. When I looked up, I was looking down the barrel of a desert eagle. "Damn Kalisha! What's up with you?!" "Don't even try it! If i'm wrong, I'm sorry!", said Kalisha. As she lowered the gun! "What? You think I wanna take yo shit?" "I'm a woman first Tory! I have to be on my P's and Q's when it comes to this. But I done opened up to you, and I'm showing you too much as it is, so you know I fuck with you and trust you." "Okay Kalisha, okay! I got you!" We stepped out of the closet, and into the guest room. "That's why I asked you what you were working with. But it doesn't matter. Yo plug gone be mad?", asked Kalisha. I laughed at that. "Nawl, I'm straight. What's this gonna cost me?" "What's the going rate for bricks on this end? But 30?", asked Kalisha. "Yeah more than likely. Probably a lil more. But they probably going to the A. which is the same." "Yeah I know.", said Kalisha. "How about 26, 5 a piece?", said Kalisha. "That's what you want?", I asked. "Sell them for that.", said Kalisha. Damn! How much of this shit she got?! "Plenty.", said Kalisha, answering my question like she's a mind reader. I just smiled at her. "That's what's up." "Look Tory, I'm not one of them square ass bitches. You been fucking with Andrea...cool,but I don't trust her. Maria..we cool, but we just hook up and do our thing. That's about to end though. Just fuck with me and you're straight!" And with that being said, I pulled her to me and kissed her. "Fuck wit you, I know you got it." Is what I said in between kisses. "Yeah bay!", said Kalisha, in between kisses. "Yeah..fuck with me you know I got it."

Chapter 8

That night, after Kalisha gave me the blow, I immediately went to work. I got on the phone and called a few niggas in Montgomery. I already knew what Vito was copping in Yayo. so I went ahead and dropped a half block on him. Sold him a quarter and fronted him one. He called a couple of niggas he knew and they bought up the rest of the dope. All in weight. Ounces, 62, 4 ways and a couple of nines. I came back with all of her money later the next day. 53 thousand. All the extra was juug money. I put it up. She was elated. "Damn baby! You done got rid of all of them?", asked Kalisha. "Yeah. you got more?" "I told you, plenty of it.", said Kalisha. She disappeared into one of her hideaways and came out with a duffle bag. "Here..check it out!", said Kalisha. "That's 14." "It's 14 keys in this bag?", I asked, like Rico Cameron on paid in full. I almost felt the impulse to do her, like Rico did mitch on Paid in Full. but nawl, I'm kind of feeling her, and I don't want any bad shit to come back on me. Karma's a bitch. Besides, I'll get more out of her by keeping it 100 with her. She knows something or somebody heavy. "I know you're wondering how I keep all this work.", said Kalisha reading my mind. "Yeah, but it ain't my business, so I'm not pushing it. I'm just curious because I'm sleeping with you and stuff. You're my girl and baby. I just want you to be careful. Icare about you!", I said as I leaned in to kiss her. "Oh you care about me?, asked Kalisha, smiling as we kissed. "Yeah baby..I care about you!" "Pouring the honey on thick, I sat the duffle bag down and embraced Kalisha, and kissed her more intently. She slightly moaned, as I gripped her ass. What a package deal. A bad ass bitch, that looks good, and is shaped like Lisa Raye, who is plugged the fuck up like a young Giselda Blanco, and she's a detective! Which could be a blessing and a curse. Her sex game is the bomb, in which I'm about to get into at this very moment. Kalisha had been working out, so she had on some black, short ass boy shorts, along with a purple sports bra, with a sheen of sweat misting her skin. As it was, her hair was pulled back in a ponytail, I grabbed it and kind of roughly pulled her head back and sucked and kissed her neck. While I was servicing her neck, she had swiftly released my throbbing tool from my jeans, and was stroking it. I let my jeans fall down as I was snatching her boy shorts down, and bending her over at the same time. "Get this pussy daddy.", whispered Kalisha, as she reached back and busted the cheeks I love open. I entered Kalisha and pulled her by her ponytail at the same time Kalisha was rolling that ass on me, throwing the pussy back like she had done popped an ecstasy pill or something. Looking back at me, eye to eye contact. Kalisha was all the way in porno mode. "Siss yess! Get this pussy baby!!", said Kalisha, pushing me over the edge, into erotic city. I cuffed my hands up under Kalisha's shoulders. I punched hard up into Kalisha until I blasted off. Kalisha was still throwing that pussy on me, working her walls, milking my unborn up out of me. "Is it good to you baby?", purred Kalisha. "Uhh-huh!", I responded. Those all the words I can manage to say at the moment. I quickly pulled my boxers and jeans up, grabbed the duffle bag, kissed Kalisha, and was headed for the door. Then I stopped. A thought hit me. "Hey baby let's go with 25 a piece." "Whatever baby.", said Kalisha. "Whatever?", I asked kind of puzzled. "What, you make this stuff or something?" "I'll hip you baby. Ii promise. Soon!", said Kalisha. "Okay." I was acting rather reluctant. And Kalisha read it. "Baby everything is cool. It ain't nothing fishy going on. I'll tell you what's up. Just be cool! Okay?" "That's what's up!", I said and hit the door. I was gone.

6 months later

Riding in Kalisha's drop top Aston Martin, high, I'm thinking about how shit changed this fast. We're on a lil mini vacation down in Miami's South Beach. I had found out 6 months ago what's really happening with Kalisha. After I moved those 14 bricks, first of all, Kalisha is Dominican. She has a brother and cousin who are DEA and another cousin on the coast guard, all who are Dominican. So when certain ships come through strapped with drugs from the Cartel, they'll let them come on in, for a nice price and drugs. Some they'll get tipped off about, and they will bust the shipment, and turn some of the dope in and keep the rest of it. And in turn, they supply friends and family. So, that's how Kalisha is so in with the dope, through her, Rouge DEA and Rouge Coastguard. Family members! But like August Alsina, "I love it!" I love it because I'm on like a magic stone. Stronger than the Holy Ghost, and is living a fulfilled desire. I'm the brick man. Plus I'm an heroin distributor and grade A weed supplier. Since I've been kicking it with Kalisha, Andrea nor Maria have heard from me as often. Both of them have been calling like hell though. One day, a couple of months ago, Andrea called, and I went ahead and answered her. "What's up?" "Heyy, how have you been doing?", said Andrea. "Um coolin..and you?" "I'm doing okay. Just wondering why you haven't been answering my calls." "Seemed to me like you needed some space or something. So that's what I'm doing.", I casually answered. "Um..who said I needed some space?' "Your actions? Look where are you now?", I asked, cutting to the chase. "At home..why?" "I'll be over there.", I said and hung up not giving her a chance to say anything. Once I got to her, she let me right in, and we went at it. I fucked Andrea in the buck, on her couch. When I was about to nut, I pulled my dick out and put it right in her mouth and blasted off. I can tell she didn't like me handling her like a slut. Yet, she swallowed it. My phone was going off like crazy, so I wasn't trying to hang around long. Besides, I was thinking about how wishy washy she'd been with me. Pulling my pants up, grabbing my phone, checking it, Andrea froze me with the look on her face. "Damn Andrea! Wassup?" "You just gone handle me like you're handling me?", asked Andrea. "What you mean?", I asked, knowing what she was talking about. "Like I don't matter? Like I'm nothing. Ever since you been fucking with Kalisha, you've been on some other type of shit Tory." With that, I got to stepping towards the door. "You wonder how I knew that huh?" I looked back at her as I was twisting the door knob and chunked the deuces up at her. "I'll holla at you Andrea." "Okay! You're going down with that bitch Tory! Just mark my word Tory! Internal affairs is all over that hoe!" Andrea was hollering at the top of her lungs. I hurried up and blew that spot. Going against my better judgment and first mind, I told Kalisha about what Andrea said. I didn't tell her that I had been over to Andrea's house fucking her. I told her that she called, and Kalisha did some crazy shit, by confronting Andrea about it and they fought like hell in the police department. I told her not to say anything and she just couldn't help herself. Maria called me and got in my shit about it. Oh well, just got to be careful. Meanwhile, I'm riding down Biscayne with the top dropped, Kalisha hit my phone with some fine ass shots of her posing in her pink 2 piece bikini. Then she sent some videos of her and one of her dominican friends hanging out. They was in the bed room on the bed getting it in. kissing on each other's necks and titties. Then digging in each other's twats. Then finally, the fine dominican woman was in between Kalisha's thighs eating her up. The chick was working her tongue like a pro making Kalisha moan and holler. But she wasn't hollering the females name, she was hollering my name. "Ooo Tory! Ttorry!" My dick was harder than Chinese arithmetic. I nearly ran off into somebody's car looking at the video. I called her. "Hello? Sisss shit! Come on Tory.", moaned Kalisha. "I'm on my way!", I said, as I put the pedal to the metal.

We was staying at the Fontainebleau Hotel, in a suite. I encountered so many bad bitches at the hotel, but my mind was on Kalisha, and that fine chick on the video. Kalisha, so official with her game, she knocked this chick off at Club LIV the night before. She caught me watching her while she was on the dance floor? "Daddy, what? You want her?", asked Kalisha. "Nawl! Why you ask me.." "Don't front baby, I seen you watching her.", said Kalisha, as she cut my answer short. "Want me to pull her for you papi?", said Kalisha in my ear. "Yeah!", I answered. Kalisha went to the dance floor and whispered in the chick's ear and she walked off the floor with Kaalisha, and the rest was history. I guess that's why I was so into her, cause she was game tight. Fine, pretty and well paid. As I eased into the hotel suite, the scent of vanilla candles invaded my nose. The lights were low and all I heard was some old school Jodeci playing, and sexy moans. I went to the bar and fixed myself a drink. Straight hennessy, no ice, no chaser. Lit me a cigarillo of some OG Kush, and watched as Kalisha and the dominican broad 69'd, eating each other's cat. After I finished my blunt and drank, I immediately got naked with condom in hand, slid my hard dick in Kalisha's mouth, interrupting her feast. The pretty ass Dominican chick opened her eyes to see what was going on and that's when I slid my middle finger into her wet tight pussy, in place of Kalisha's tongue. Like a real porno star, I replaced my middle finger, with my spit shined dick into the Dominican chicks pussy. Only for a couple of strokes though. Only enough to get her juices on my rod and once I took it out, Kalisha was on it. "Damn baby! You my nasty girl!", I whispered to Kalisha, as she slurped me down. The Dominican girl was thirsty for me to go up in her, after teasing her. "Uh uh papi. More!", moaned the Dominican broad, as she grabbed my dick. "Hold it.", I said as I slid my rubber on. I wasn't about to hit it raw. I moved Kalisha up out the way and ran up in the Dominican chick. As I was getting my smash on, Kalisha straddled the chick's face and was like Shawna's old song, "Gettin some head!"

Chapter 9

Everything is going good with me and Kalisha's business so far. We moving about five to ten bricks a week through Montgomery, Alabama, as a base of operations, to the surrounding areas. Going to Birmingham and selling a few dudes ounces of heroin a couple of times a week. Pounds and pounds of exotic weed and bales of mid grade weed. Got a white boy I move ice through. I still was living in Atlanta, so I moved a lot of dope there. I bought me a big ass house out in Lithonia and a nice crib in Montgomery, Alabama in Deer Park community. I still had my Cadillac, but I had done upgraded to a Bentley coupe, drop top. I normally didn't drive it in Montgomery, but one sunny weekend, I did. I came through with the top dropped and what did I do that for? Andrea was on duty at and I was coming down Carter Hill Road, turning on Hall Street/Harris way, and she was at the red light, by the liberty gas station at the intersection. When I turned on Hall Street, we looked at each other and she did a double take, like "What the fuck?!" All the shit she had said to me that night after I handled her like a slut, invaded my memory. I thought she was going to keep going, but she turned around. "What the fuck is she doing?", I said to the empty car, as I watched her through the rearview mirror. It was three carrs separating Andrea and me. I don't know what she's up to, but she's killing my vibe. I'm riding through the campus, about to get my flex on to see which one of these young hot mommas I could fuck today. But now, it might be a change of plans. The speed bumps were slowing me up, and it was one before I got to the next turn. One of the three cars had took a right turn, before going over the first speed bump, now it's two. When I got to the left turn, I was held up again because of a student crossing! It must been in the middle of changing classes, judging by the traffic of students. It was a lot of fine young females crossing, and a few of them was waving and flirting. Admiring me and my foreign drop top. Any other time, I would've been flirting back, trying to knock something off, but now wasn't the time. It was a campus police on the scene directing traffic and he finally allowed me to take the left, and when I did, Andrea was right there on my ass because the other two cars went straight. I made a complete stop at the stop sign. I pulled up on the hill, on the side of the acadome, to the next stop sign, by the cafeteria, and that's when it happened. Andrea pulled the lights on me! "Damn! What is wrong with this bitch?!", I said to myself, because I haven't done anything wrong. Andrea is on the bullshit! I turned my music down to see what's on her mind, as she approached the Bentley. "What's up Andrea? What did I do wrong?", I innocently asked Andrea because I truly did nothing wrong! "Step out of the car.", said Andrea in her robo cop voice. Now this shit is getting scary. I stepped out of the car. "Damn baby...what's up?", I said with an attitude. Andrea's nostrils had flared and she had fire in her eyes! "Whose car is this?", she asked. "It's mine." "Can I see some license and registration?" Now she's acting up. Harassing me like she doesn't know me or something. I paused for a minute, giving her this look like "Bitch, you trippin!" "Did you not understand what I asked you?", said Andrea. "Yeah, I understood! I'm just trying to see why you tripping?" "Sir, are you resisting?" Andrea was most definitely on some more shit, so I complied with her and went to the dashboard and got my registration, etc. she went back to her car and checked things out. Now I'm fuming. Leaning against my car on the phone calling Kalisha. "Don't you know that this crazy bitch Andrea got me pulled over on Alabama State campus?" "For what?!", asked Kalisha. "Nothing!!", I said. "She on some hating type shit!" "What is she doing now?", asked Kalisha. "Just sitting in her car like she's reading something." "You don't have anything on you do you? Because just radioed for some back up! Specifically the drug dogs." "You serious?!", I asked, "Because I'm not believing my ears." "Yes I'm serious! I heard it over the scanner. I'm on my way.", said Kalisha. I hit end on my phone, and looked back at Andrea to see what she was up to. She still had her head down. That's when I text her phone, but it wouldn't go through. Then I called her. "The number you've called has been changed or no longer in service." Damn! She done changed her number! Everything that Andrea had said that night is replaying in my head, and to top it off, I look up and see the cavalry coming. A couple of detective cars, suburban with big white boys hanging all off the side. Jump street! With the drug sniffing dogs in the lead, like a pace car, in a car race. That's when Andrea got out of her. "Andrea..wassup with all this shit!", I asked her. She wouldn't say nothing until them dog folks and the rest of the cops pulled up. "Hey y'all! I had got a tip that he might be trafficking drugs, and probably would be taking them to Alabama State University. So when I seen this car, it fit the description. Smell like he's been smoking marijuana also", said Andrea, as she smirked at me. I could spit in her face right now, I'm so pissed. True, I had been smoking, but it was gone now. But I know the dog is going to hit somewhere and that somewhere was on my first. "Sir, do you have any drugs on you?" "No sir..I don't. Your dog might be a little hungry. I just ate and the smell is probably still on me.", I said being sarcastic. "Yeah right.", said the officer. "Oh..he's an ex convict also! So you might have to strip search him! You know all the stories we've heard about prisoners!", said Andrea. "I'm not a prisoner!", I said. But I wanted to say, "When I was a prisoner, I used to fuck you all on your desk!" But I chilled. Now they had the nasty ass drug dog all in my Bentley! He was barking, alerting them to the driver's side of my car. They searched and searched but didn't come up with nothing. "Is there a bathroom around here?", asked one of the officers. "Yeah! Take him in the Acadome.", said Andrea. I couldn't believe Andrea. She wants me to be humiliated! "Where in the fuck is Kalisha?", I was thinking, and that's when she pulled up. "Where are you taking him?", asked Kalisha, as she was getting out of the car." To strip search him.", said another officer. "That won't be necessary.", said Kalisha. The police was looking towards his comrades for help, and was attempting to say something. "But detective." "If he isn't under arrest for anything, and you all haven't found anything yet, let him go.", interrupted Kalisha. "Officer Stevens, what kind of probable cause did you have to stop him?" By now Andrea is fuming and I am smiling. "I had a tip that he was trafficking drugs.", slowly said Andrea through clenched teeth. "Okay...did your tip come from a reliable source?", asked Kalisha. "You know what? Fuck it!", said Andrea. "Just be ready to answer to internal affairs for.." "Officer Steens you have some type of problem!", said Kalisha, cutting Andrea off, and almost stepping to her, before a couple of officers stepped between them. That's when Andrea hopped in her police car, turned her blue flashers off, and took off. A couple of the officers on the scene was confused, but a couple kind of thought they had a clue about what was going on, especially if they heard about their fight at the station a while back. "Sir, you're free to go!", said Kalisha as she hopped in her detective car, and mashed out. The rest of the cops was getting into their cars and a couple of them was smirking at me. "Nice car.", said one of the smirkers.

"What you think that bitch is up to?", I asked Maria. "I don't know! Whatever it is, it ain't good!" Maria had called me, once she heard about what happened over on ASU campus. "I mean...I know she is hating on you and kalisha's relationship or whatever, but hear me out..the word is that she's been hanging out with internal affairs, and the feds." "Internal affairs?", I repeated. "She mentioned something about internal affairs to me one night. In a threatening manner!" "Whaat?! You've been still fucking with her?", said Maria. "Once.", I said. "Well she was always hating after we hooked up those times. I mean she was looking at you like you were her man!" "You feel me?" "So when you started straying away from her, she was feeling some type of way. Mad at herself because one of her unfulfilled desires backfires on her. She can't respect it. And when she found out that you was fucking with Kalisha heavy...exclusively?! She got pisssed! Because she hates Kalisha!" Maria was in rare form now. Rapidly spitting out her words. Her hispanic, dialogue kicks in overdrive when she's hype. "Okay...how does she know about me and Kalisha?", I asked, slowing Maria down. "Simple...she heard me and Kalisha talking about you one day when we were in the break room. I had told Kalisha that you and Andrea had a lil something going on and Kalisha being the person she is, she kind of rubbed things, in by slipping up and saying your name or something!" "Then I don;t know what the feds have to do with it, but something wasn't right!" "Feds?", I asked. "Yeah! Feds as in FBI!",said Maria. Now my mind is running 100 miles per hour trying to figure out what was really going on. Feds investigation?

"Internal affairs? They're the ones to investigate cos or something?"
"Yeah....especially if they feel like that cop is going astray!", said Maria.
"Okay, thanks for keeping me posted Maria!" "Okay!" I hung up with
Maria and called Kalisha to discuss the rising problem. The internal
affairs, is her problem, but the feds?? We've got to find where the
leak is. After talking to Kalisha about this bullshit, I felt drained and
spooked. She is convinced that everything is going to be okay, and to
let her handle it. I know all day, all my people I'm dealing with is solid.
I had to go through with convincing her of that, by letting her know
that nobody knows that my plug is the police. That's why internal
affairs is in the investigation, because the flaw is coming from her end
somewhere! Just like that, and I was right.

Chapter 10

2 weeks after the run in with Andrea over at ASU, Kalisha and I were scheduled to go to Los Angeles for a pick up. What was supposed to be a business trip turned into another mini vacation, due to Kalisha's brothers and company delay of plans. We got there on a Wednesday. Supposingly to cop our work, on that Thursday and back on a flight, heading back to Montgomery, Alabama that Friday. Beating the dope back. However, it was Friday, and we still hadn't cored. While we were waiting on the green light from her brother, we went over to the rodeo drive and did some shopping. After that, we went out to a trendy restaurant where stars frequently go a lot, rode around Hollywood and went to a couple of clubs. Took and posted pics like crazy on facebook at all those spots, and went back to the Ritz Carlton and fucked like crazy. We didn't hear from her brothers till Sunday. The ship they were waiting on had a couple of days delayed due to the weather. Once the ship arrived, the Rogue DEA boys did their thing and called us the following day, and that's when the beginning of the end, seed was planted.

One of Kalisha's brother, Henchmen got collared by the FBI and the FBI internal affairs undercover down in St. Petersburg, Florida, without anybody knowing. The Henchmen, is a DEA agent himself. Just lower in rank than Kalisha's brother. But he is in the Rogue circle. He has a friend who is on the force in St. Petersburg. A hero of sorts within the force, after he was shot in the line of duty, and survived. The DEA agent had been friends with this guy since middle school, so it was easy for him to be set up by him, because he confided in him like a brother. When he tried to bring him in on the illegal business, this guy set the DEA agent up, thinking he was doing the right thing morally. With that happening, he was now setting up Kalisha's brother's operation. He's cooperating with the government, internal affairs, and the US Attorney General's office. The bad thing is that shit rolls down hill. They want everybody involved. So when the government got Kalisha's brother's phone tapped, and my phone also! This is the shit Andrea was screaming about! Internal affairs once they caught wind of Kalisha's involvement, they started questioning the police in Atlanta Police Department, and the Montgomery Police department. When they questioned Andrea, asking her what did she know about Kalisha, she told them Kalisha's involvement with me! An ex con drug dealer! When Kalisha's brother called her and told her the location for us to meet them, and when I told my people where to bring the 18 wheeler, the feds, the DEA, internal affairs, were listening to our conversations. Amazingly, they let us load the work on our truck, and trailed it all the way back to Montgomery, Alabama. Had some agents on the flight with me and Kalisha all the way back to Montgomery. Once we got back, and the work made it to our fake warehouse, everything still seemed as safe and going according to plans until the next fateful day. That night after me and Kalisha made sure everything was put up and secure, we separated for about an hour and a half, and hooked up later in a suite downtown at the Renaissance Hotel. We both knew how to move good enough to shake any tails or surveillance...so we thought. Andrea knew where we hid at times when I'm in Montgomery, and that was in Barrington Place Condos and townhouses on the far East side. At times, a security guard is placed in a lil guard shack. That night, Andrea had played the security guard into letting her hide in there. So when I came through, she was on me. She waited to see which way I turned, then hopped in an undercover and followed me from a distance. Me and Kalisha had started going to the Renaissance, about 3 months into the relationship. I liked to get a suite on the top floor at night. I loved the way the colorful lights be like strobe lights flashing! They be illuminating the room if the lights are off, and the blinds open. I loved to bend Kalisha over, and fuck her looking out of the window over the city, as the colored lights shined on us. We were laying back in the bed chilling, watching TV and some breaking news came on. WSFA Breaking News Report. "Hi, I'm Sally Fitz, reporting live from Montgomery. We're here at this warehouse on Hayneville Road with the Federal Bureau of Investigations, the DEA, internal affairs for both agencies, along with the Montgomery police department. A sting has unfolded as the authorities search the warehouse. Cocaine, heroin, and high grades of marijuana had been seized."..me and Kalisha looked at each other stunned. "A source close to the investigation said authorities believe that a warehouse in Los Angeles, California, was also searched, and a ton of cocaine, 20 keys of heroin, and 200 pounds of high grade marijuana, with an estimated street value of 4 or 500 million dollars! It appeared that some Rogue DEA officers were caught in the warehouse with drugs and a cache of weapons. This was part of the sting in which a warehouse here in Montgomery. Suspects are sought in this care and more arrests are expected.." We were astonished. We laid there for a minute in total quietness. "We got to get out of here!", I said breaking the silence. "Wait!", said Kalisha as she grabbed my dick. "What are you doing?! We got to get out of here baby!" "Baby they don't know we're here! Let's make love one more time before we leave.", said Kalisha. I think that she knows that this might be the final curtain call for us. My dick wouldn't work at first. I'm so full of anxiety! She put her lips on it and started to suck it till it started to rise. As she was getting me right, we was in for a surprise. Andrea bent the corner with a pistol in hand. "Freeze!", she calmly said. "Freeze?! Bitch what the fuck are you doing in my room?!" I exploded before I knew it. "Bitch this is what you mad about?!", asked Kalisha, referring to my dick still in her hand. "You both are under arrest!", said Andrea. We didn't know if she was serious or not, because she was without backup. At least not at this point. "Jealous, crazy, stalking ass bitch!", screamed Kalisha, as she rose up off of the bed, that's when Andrea shot Kalisha! "Bam bam!" Two quick shots to the abdomen. Then got on her earpiece walkie talkie. "Wanted drug suspects located at the Renaissance Hotel, suite number 17, 12th floor, shots fired!" That's when she fired two more shots at me hitting me in the right shoulder and right thigh. "Officer need assistance!" That's when she reached in her right pocket and pulled out a throwaway pistol. A little .32 automatic, ran over to the bed where me and Kalisha was, snatched Kalisha's hand from covering her bleeding wound, and put the pistol in her hand, and squeezed the trigger. Making it look as if Kalisha shot her in her right thigh! Really grazing it. That's when she shot Kalisha dead between her eyes. Blowing Kalisha's brain out and spitting in her face. I knew it was over then. Andrea reached in her left pocket and pulled out a small .380 and forced it into my hands, trying to make me shoot her in the leg. "Muthafucka you gone pay! Squeeze the trigger Tory!", said Andrea. I dropped the pistol. "Fine! You don't have to do it!" I'm still going to be justified in shooting your no good criminal ass!", said Andrea as she stood over me, shedding tears with her fingers, massaging the trigger, aiming at my head and then ..."Boom!"

To Be Continued...

Chapter 9

"We ain't going steady"

Chapter 31

About Author

Author Corey Bryant is 50 yrs old. Corey was born in Opelika, Alabama. As a child, Corey enjoyed reading all kinds of books and magazines. At the age of 19, Corey was incarcerated in the state of Alabama Prison System. After serving about 3 years he started writing, but didn't get serious about it until after serving about 20 years. That's when he wrote and completed yielding to unfair desires volume one and part of volume two and Rico volume one Corey still enjoys reading, writing and spending time with his family and friends. Corey resides with his family in Opelika, Alabama.